Sugar h... ..., ... eyes full of impish pleasure as she popped the piece into her mouth, then closed her eyes to enjoy it.

He wasn't sure, but Jackson thought he might just have fallen in love, with her mouth if nothing else. She mystified and fascinated him. Before he'd met her, he wouldn't have put the words innocent and sensual together, but she embodied them both. Her sensuality was just about the only innocent thing about her—she was guilty as sin when it came to the part she played in his captivity.

She tore off another piece and raised it toward her lips, then noticed him again. "I'm sorry— would you like some?" she asked, holding the fruit out to him.

He could easily have refused, but this woman was irresistible. Without another thought beyond the one that he wanted to touch her with his mouth, steal a kiss however he could, he bent his head and took the fruit from her hand, his teeth grazing the tips of her fingers.

She made a small gasp as her lips parted in surprise, and he wondered: could it be love?

WHAT ARE *LOVESWEPT* ROMANCES?

They are stories of true romance and touching emotion. We believe those two very important ingredients are constants in our highly sensual and very believable stories in the LOVESWEPT line. Our goal is to give you, the reader, stories of consistently high quality that may sometimes make you laugh, sometimes make you cry, but are always fresh and creative and contain many delightful surprises within their pages.

Most romance fans read an enormous number of books. Those they truly love, they keep. Others may be traded with friends and soon forgotten. We hope that each LOVESWEPT romance will be a treasure—a "keeper." We will always try to publish

LOVE STORIES YOU'LL NEVER FORGET
BY AUTHORS YOU'LL ALWAYS REMEMBER

The Editors

Loveswept® 726

DRAGON'S EDEN

GLENNA McREYNOLDS

BANTAM BOOKS
NEW YORK · TORONTO · LONDON · SYDNEY · AUCKLAND

To MTP in CA for all
the TLC

DRAGON'S EDEN

A Bantam Book / February 1995

ISBN 0-553-44487-5

Published simultaneously in the United States and Canada

PRINTED IN THE UNITED STATES OF AMERICA

OPM   0 9 8 7 6 5 4 3 2 1

AUTHOR'S NOTE

Dear Reader,

Dragon's Eden is a story of innocence and temptation, of exile and forgiveness. For my Treasured Tale, I've reached beyond folklore and myth to an archetype of love, Adam and Eve in the Garden of Eden.

My dragon's Eden is a lush, tropical island caressed by sunlight and nourished with rain, a place of abundant life nurtured by both a divine and human hand. There are reptiles, real, mythical, and disguised, wild, enticing, and savage, and all are dangerous—especially to the untouched woman trapped in paradise.

In this Eden, the Tree of Life and the Tree of Knowledge take the form of many trees, endangered species from the rain forest that are cultivated on the island in hopes they may save humankind.

Above all, the Garden is a place where love may flower with desire, but finds its full blossoming in compassion.

So come through the pirate's door into *Dragon's Eden*, where primordial man arose from the sea and was welcomed into paradise, however reluctantly, by a fallen angel seeking forgiveness for her sins.

My best to you,

PROLOGUE

The island floated on the horizon in a darkly azure sea, its windward edge painted into visibility by the rising sun. Jackson Daniels leaned closer to the seaplane's window, watching the blush of dawn spread up the eastern flank of a tall, jagged mountain. Morning mists wreathed the peak with gossamer clouds and liquid sunshine, making the island look like paradise, a tropical heaven on earth.

He turned away from the window, letting out a short sound of disgust. Given the way his luck had been running lately, his money was on the island being just a new version of hell.

He looked down at the shackles on his ankles, the handcuffs on his wrists, and the chain running between the two inconveniences. It didn't matter what the island turned out to be, he wasn't going anywhere, neither to heaven nor hell without his jailer's permission. That was for damn sure.

2

The plane banked, and Sher Chang, the brutish behemoth sitting next to him, jerked him back from the window, grabbing him by his wounded shoulder and digging his fingers in hard. A curse lodged against Jackson's teeth. From the seat in front of him, he heard a woman's murmured command to release him. Sher Chang complied, and Jackson slumped forward into a silent ball of pain.

He knew from experience that any show of weakness on his part would be met with a generous dose of injected painkillers, just as any show of strength was met with an added shackle and chain. He couldn't win. He'd been at the mercy of the woman and her gang of Chinese pirates since . . . since forever, it seemed.

A wry grin curved his mouth. The situation could have been worse. Instead of the young woman named Sun Shulan sitting in the front seat of the seaplane, his jailer could have been her mother, Fang Baolian, dreaded pirate queen of the South China Sea and the lady who'd had him shot for refusing her sexual favors.

"Stop worrying, Jen. You're like an old woman," Shulan said in Cantonese, her voice rising enough for Jackson to hear her over the drone of the engines. She sounded exasperated with the old man in the seat next to her. "She will accept him onto the island, and she will take care he is not harmed. I can do no better for him than to bring him here, away from Hong Kong and my mother's spies."

She? Jackson thought, his body tensing in spite of himself. He didn't need another "she." He didn't want another "she" running and ruining his life. He'd always known maritime bounty hunting was dangerous work—pirates had only gotten more daring and more ruthless over the centuries, not less—but he'd never thought it would be a woman who finally brought him to his knees, let alone three: Baolian, the "hell has no fury like a woman scorned" contingent; Shulan, the one who had saved him for reasons he'd rather not believe; and now the new "she," the one who would take him and keep him on a small strip of land floating between the earth and the sky.

He, the hunter, had been trapped by women, captured by women. His only consolation was in knowing his brother, Cooper, had survived Baolian's ambush on the godforsaken beach south of Singapore where he'd been shot. Shulan had sworn that was true, and Jackson believed the pirate princess. It was easy to believe her when she held his hands in hers and gazed at him with her warm amber eyes, her expression sweetly innocent, assuring him she only had his welfare at heart. It was harder to believe her when she had an extra chain added to his bindings. He wished she would hurry up and ransom him, get the whole ordeal over with. He could imagine no other reason for her interference in her mother's fit of deadly pique, despite her wild story of him being her long-lost half brother.

The plane dropped in altitude, making a slow descent into the mist. Within seconds, they were enshrouded in impenetrable fog. The mountain and the island's rolling green hills were gone, along with the azure sea and the streaking brilliance of dawn across the horizon.

An unexpected calm overtook him in those silent moments of blind flying, a peace he shouldn't have felt. Maybe it was merely acceptance of the inevitable, but it felt like something more, like a promise of life, or joy.

The fanciful thought brought another wry grin to his lips. Joy. Right. He was losing it.

"Sedate him," Shulan ordered, and his peace shattered.

He swore, a vicious sound that had no effect whatsoever on his jailers. He felt the prick of the needle and the flood of warmth that always preceded a deep, dreamless sleep.

"When he's out, take off the cuffs and chains, and be careful with him." Shulan's voice came to him as if from a far distance. "If he drowns in the surf, I'll turn you all over to my mother."

Hell, he decided in one last hazy thought. Not life. Not joy. The island was going to be pure hell.

ONE

Sugar Caine stood next to the wicker chair closest to the bed, her gaze traveling the length of the man sprawled facedown across the tumbled disarray he'd made of her sheets. He was naked and beautiful . . . so beautiful, his body intrinsically sensual, a tawny, seductive landscape of lean, muscled curves and hard planes. Just looking at him started a wave of longing in her heart. She'd been alone for so long.

Jackson was his name. *Jack Sun.* His dark hair fell forward, hiding his face and draping his shoulder before disappearing underneath him. Sunlight filtering through the jalousies that covered the leeward windows made stripes of light and darkness across his broad back, but most of his body was veiled by the deepening shadows of a Caribbean afternoon. The soles of his feet were callused, as were the palms of his hands. One shoulder was bandaged with white gauze, and the rest of him was simply perfect.

A soft groan escaped him, a breath of pain as he shifted. Concern drew Sugar's brows together. She leaned forward ever so slightly, ready to help him if he needed help, even while she prayed he wouldn't. She didn't want to touch him. She didn't dare. She couldn't afford to get that close to so much trouble, and he was trouble of the worst kind, a magnet for danger, a man marked for murder by Fang Baolian.

With the grace and languor of a slowly awakening animal, he rolled onto his back, sending a silky cascade of ebony hair sliding across his torso. The dark strands reached his waist, curving across his sleekly muscled chest and abdomen like a river of black satin. She'd wondered how long his hair was. When Shulan's men had carried him up from the beach at dawn, it had been impossible to tell. The sky had still been too dark, his hair tangled in his ragged clothes. Her concern then had been more for his vital signs than his physical attributes.

She wished she could still say the same. Her gaze lifted to his face, and she felt warmth bloom in her cheeks. He was easily as beautiful as his half sister, Sun Shulan, and equally exotic, a rare blend of East and West. Thick black lashes fringed his closed eyes. His eyebrows were dark with a slight curve, more like a red-tailed hawk's wings than a shorebird's. She wasn't surprised. Even wounded and sound asleep, he had the aura of a predator.

The blush she wouldn't have admitted to for the world deepened as her gaze strayed to the juncture of his thighs. He *was* beautiful, his hair there silky and dark, his manhood glorious. Chastising herself, she reached down and pulled the top sheet up to his waist, for all the good it did her. A moment later he'd worked the sheet back off.

"That boy, he likes being naked, Sugar."

Sugar took a moment to clear her throat before she agreed with her friend. "I know, Carolina," she said, looking up at the tall black woman standing in the open doorway.

"You want I should tell your papa that boy is here?" Carolina asked, tying a bow in the yellow sash belting her tangerine-colored dress.

"No. Not yet." Sugar knew Dr. Thomas Caine would be apoplectic if he knew his daughter was harboring a bounty hunter who had crossed Fang Baolian. It would remind him too much of her youthful mistakes and a past best forgotten—though it could never truly be forgotten.

"I don' know why they brought that boy here," Carolina said. She tilted her head and clipped a large tangerine-and-yellow earring on one ear. "It don' make no sense, no how. They should've taken him to Kingstown and let your papa have him."

Sugar had told her old friend as much, but Shulan had assured her that the man she called half brother wasn't in danger of dying. He'd been treated by the finest doctors in Hong Kong and spent weeks recuperating there before Shulan had transported him halfway around the world to the Caribbean. He did need care and watching over, but nothing beyond Sugar's skills.

Mostly he needed protection, Shulan had said, protection and confinement—for his own good.

Sugar had understood what was being asked of her: repayment of a debt left too long unpaid. Shulan had given Sugar a sanctuary when she'd most needed it. In return for that salvation, the pirate princess wanted her to hold this man at Cocorico Bay, Sugar's refuge at the end of the world, where her home hugged sheer rock walls and the sea offered the only escape.

She wasn't so sure Shulan had been right about her half brother's health. The only sign of life he'd given all day, besides his breathing and occasional movement, had happened between the time when Shulan and her cohorts had left him fully clothed on the bed and a half hour later, when Carolina had gone in to check on him and let out a little scream of shocked sensibilities.

What would possess an injured man to use his last ounce of strength to take his clothes off was beyond Sugar's understanding. Unless, even injured and drugged, the pile of coolie clothes they'd found at the foot of the bed had offended him as much as they had offended Carolina. Carolina had immediately carried them over to the cabana and dumped them in the rag-bag, grumbling about having no bondslaves on Cocorico.

"If he hasn't wakened by morning, I'll make sure he gets to St. Vincent," Sugar told Carolina. She wondered if Shulan knew what lengths she might have to go for the stranger's life, what risks might be involved. She hadn't been back to Kingstown since she'd left with the fear of God in her heart.

"Your papa isn't gonna like this. He isn't gonna like any of this," Carolina warned, clipping on her other earring.

"I know. That's why we're not telling him, or Momma either."

"What about that man?" Carolina asked, gesturing toward the courtyard.

Sugar shook her head in resignation. She didn't know anything about the ancient, fragile-looking man Shulan had left at Cocorico, except he was Chinese and he was there to protect Jackson.

As she returned her attention to the man stretched out on the bed, a few quaint sayings went through her mind. Ones about chickens coming home to roost and reaping what you've sown. She'd learned a long time ago that some mistakes lasted a lifetime. The stranger on her bed was proof of that.

"I don' like the look of the old Chinee," Carolina went on. "You want I should stay?"

"No." Sugar glanced at her friend. "You go on back to Kingstown. I'll be fine. If it makes you feel better, have Henry come back in the morning."

"Henry." Carolina gave a ladylike snort. "That man good for nothin' at all."

Despite her friendship with the old sailor, Sugar couldn't disagree. Henry, sweet as he was, was truly good for nothing. Too many years of rum and sunshine had taken all the gumption out of him.

"I jus don' like leaving you with a foreign devil and a naked boy. That's all."

If the man on the bed had been a boy, Sugar would

have had far fewer doubts herself. As for the foreign
devil standing guard in the courtyard . . . She glanced
out the open doorway at the old man staring at the sea.
If a good wind didn't blow him over, she'd count herself
lucky. If a good wind did blow him over, then she'd
have some explaining to do.

Letting out an exasperated sigh, Carolina strode forward and snapped the sheet up over the sleeping man's
body. Then she bent down and tucked the sheet under
the mattress. "If this don' hold him, nothin' will," she
grumbled, walking around the end of the bed to do the
same to the other side. "I swear, I've only covered this
boy five times today. I ain't never seen—"

She stopped cold, the sudden halt in her speech
bringing Sugar's head up. Carolina had gone pale beneath the café au lait color of her skin. She dropped the
sheet and took a step back from the bed, crossing herself.

"Sweet God A'mighty," she murmured. "Obeahman."

Obeahman? Sugar turned to stare at the man on the
bed. One look at where the river of his hair had flowed
onto the bed, revealing the left side of his chest, was all
she needed to see to know why Carolina suddenly held
him in fear, why she thought he was a sorcerer of the
island magic, obeah.

Sugar was a bit more skeptical, despite his elaborate
tattoo.

"There are no white obeahmen, Carolina," she said
dryly.

"There was, missy," the older woman scolded as she crossed herself again. "Once they had a white obeahman on St. Lucia. I seen him myself."

"I saw him too. He wasn't white."

"White enough," Carolina said, arching an aristocratic eyebrow in her direction. "Jus' like this boy."

Sugar tried another tack. "This man came here from Hong Kong. Who would go to Hong Kong to get an obeahman?"

"Nobody with no sense, that's for sure." The older woman huffed.

Sugar nodded in agreement. "This man is no obeahman."

"Well, he sure is something," Carolina insisted.

Sugar agreed with that, too, but she wasn't sure what name to put to him—until she looked again at his tattoo.

"He's a dragon man, Carolina, and dragon men have no power in the lower latitudes."

Carolina rolled her eyes and cast a droll look in Sugar's direction. "You, missy, got so much to learn, it ain't even funny."

Sugar pressed her lips together to keep from grinning.

"What you know about men fit on the head of a pin, girl. What you know about dragon men you don' even need a pin to hold."

Sugar's lips twitched.

"Don' you go grinnin' at me, missy. You may be too big to have your bottom paddled, but that don' mean I might not try." Carolina turned her attention to the man on the bed, leaning over and taking a good long look at the tattoo emblazoned on his left breast. "Why this here is nothin' more than a naked dragon boy," she said in a dismissive tone, rising to stand tall and straight next to the bed. "If'n he gives you any trouble, you call your papa."

"I will," Sugar promised, her gaze straying to the sleeping man.

Her smile faded. He was already giving her trouble, just by lying there. Without another move he was an added misadventure in a life she'd tried damn hard to keep on the straight and narrow.

He kicked at the sheet, and a softly muttered curse rose from his lips. Sugar felt her heart sink lower in her chest. Lord help her. She had a dragon man in her bed, a beautiful, dangerous, fascinating dragon man.

Jackson woke slowly, drifting in and out of consciousness and confusion. His first realization was that he'd been drugged again, and he swore it would be the last time. Next time the bastards could just kill him and get it over with.

Right. A grin graced his mouth, and he let out a short laugh. His self-righteousness had a habit of drawing the line at actual death. He was definitely not martyr material.

He stretched, lifting one arm above his head and lengthening his torso. Damn, he wished he could open his eyes. They felt as if they'd been weighted down, but he knew that side effect of the drug would soon pass. All he had to do was wait.

His grin returned. Waiting had never been his strong suit, and he'd already waited long enough for his body to heal. Shulan had taken him on a hell of a ride, but it was time to get off before she did something terrible, like run back to her momma using him as a peace offering.

He tilted his head back to loosen the tightness in his neck, and a sigh escaped him. God, he wanted to go home.

Sugar stood transfixed in the doorway, holding a water pitcher in her hand, mesmerized by the slow stretch and release of his muscles and the play of emotions across his face. His frown had been brief, while his smile kept returning, as if it couldn't be contained. The pleased curve of his mouth was at once both sensual and wry, revealing straight white teeth and an unexpected confidence.

She knew what drugs he'd been given, and he should be waking in a state of weakness and confusion. Instead he looked like the picture of health. It was disconcerting to realize she'd waited the rest of the afternoon and part of the night for him to wake, only to find that when the moment arose, she wasn't prepared to deal with him.

He laughed again, and the soft, deep sound rolled over her like a heat wave. She'd never seen anything like him—an animal as fresh and beautiful as God's new day, uncoiling from sleep with grace, supple muscles stretching, his smile spreading.

His thick-as-sin lashes were still fanned across his cheeks, though, and that bothered her. Not being able to open his eyes must be an aftereffect she hadn't been told about. He didn't seem distressed by the hindrance, far from it. The way he laughed made her think he was as content as a cat, in love with the night whether he could see it or not. His laughter made her feel that she'd missed something wonderful, that the hours, and the moonlight, and the clouds slipping across the sky knew a particular mystery they had shared only with him.

She could believe a woman would shoot him for walking away from her bed. He was magnificent.

She moved slightly to redistribute the weight of the pitcher, then froze as he stilled on the bed, every muscle tensed, every sense alert. He was a predator readying for the kill. The only movement was the beat of his pulse, showing in the veins outlined against the hard curves of his arms. His eyes hadn't opened, but she felt as if he were staring right through her to where her heart had suddenly stopped.

In the next instant his countenance changed. He cocked his head, sending a fall of hair sliding across his chest. A look of confusion drew the winged curves of his eyebrows closer together.

"Woman?" he asked, his voice a husky counterpart to the easiness of his laughter.

She hadn't given him a clue, not one. She'd done nothing but stand in the doorway, and yet he knew. For a second the thought that Carolina might have been right about his magical powers crossed her mind. Just as quickly, she dismissed the idea. He was a bounty hunter with a dragon tattoo. Nothing more—and nothing less.

"Yes," she said, tightening her hold on the pitcher, hoping her answer would keep him from coming off the bed. She'd been going in and out of his room all evening. It hadn't occurred to her that she might need protection from him.

"But not Shulan," he said, sounding surprised but not disappointed.

"No."

"Where is she?"

"Gone."

It seemed to be the answer he expected.

"So you are the new 'she.' My new keeper?"

Sugar nodded, despite his confusing statement. Then she realized her mistake and spoke. "Yes."

A smile eased across his mouth. He came up on his elbows, looking for all the world as if he were assessing her. "And what are your plans for me, island woman?"

His tone suggested a world of possibilities Sugar wasn't about to entertain, not with him looking so incredibly at home in her bed.

"Shulan left another man," she said in warning.

His smile retreated into wryness. "The ancient one? Jen Ch'eng?"

"He hasn't introduced himself, but yes, he is very old."

"It's Jen," he said, this time sounding disappointed but not surprised. With a sigh, he relaxed back onto the bed. "Better Jen than Sher Chang, though. That steroided bastard hurt me one too many times."

She felt a flash of anger at his words. She'd sensed the huge man's cruelty. Shulan lived in the kind of world where men like Sher Chang were necessary, but Sugar would not have allowed him to stay on her island.

"Do you have anything to drink?" her patient asked. "I'm thirsty."

She glanced down at the full pitcher. Maybe he was a magic man.

Eyeing him carefully, she walked over to the bedside table and reached for a glass. Before she could lift it off the table, his hand snaked around her wrist and closed tightly. The water pitcher dropped from her other hand, landing hard on the table and splashing water on the cloth. Sugar gasped, more at the suddenness of his attack than at any pain he was inflicting.

"Don't scream," he said, pushing himself up with his free hand and swinging his legs over the side of the bed.

"There's no one to scream for," she gritted out between her teeth, furious with herself for having been caught, and by a blind man at that. She tested his grip with a quick jerk of her arm. He jerked back, coming to his feet and bringing her flush up against his body.

Her heart stopped a second time.

They were standing toe-to-toe, his knees meeting her thighs, his chest rising and falling in front of her nose. He was taller than she'd thought, more powerful —and more dangerous.

"No one?" he asked. "On the whole island?"

She wasn't going to answer. He'd find out the truth soon enough.

"What about Jen? Or are you as much his prisoner as I am?" he asked, his voice silky and arrogant. His victory over her had been quick and all too easy. "I don't know what he'd do to you, but I'm sure he'd love to have an excuse to stick another needle in me."

"You were drugged for your own protection." She repeated the words she'd been told, though had it been up to her, she would have found another way to control him.

"At least you've got part of it right," he said.

A gull's screech shattered the quietness of the night, and the man holding her reacted with the speed of a lightning strike, tightening his grip on her and whirling toward the sound in a half crouch. His hair moved in a silken wave to slide down his back. They stood motionless for the space of a breath. When he straightened and turned to her again, she was face-to-face with the dragon.

Startled, she attempted a retreat, but Jackson's hand held her firm, keeping her within the dragon's domain.

The creature's emerald-green eyes regarded her with remarkable possessiveness from across the tawny expanse of her captor's chest, but whether the dragon possessed him or wanted to possess her, she couldn't tell. She only felt the power of the lifelike image gracing the man's body from his left shoulder down to his waist. Wings held the creature aloft. Green-and-blue scales arced along its serpentine spine. Flames licked from the beast's mouth, both red and gold, warming the skin above where the man's heart lay.

Dragon fire, Sugar thought, wondering at the heat

such a creature could bring forth, wondering about the man who could contain it.

"You're smaller than I thought," he said, his grip loosening the barest of degrees.

The softer sound of his voice brought her gaze up to his, and her breath caught in her throat. He had opened his eyes. They were the color of the dragon's, but warmer, much warmer, with amber highlights and streaks of a darker brown. His thumb caressed the inside of her wrist, and her pulse leaped into overdrive.

Jackson let his gaze trail over the woman's face, and the confusion he'd felt upon waking returned. She was very unusual looking, intriguing, almost familiar. The shape of her face was feminine, a delicate heart, but her features were more childlike, rounded and less defined, suggesting an innocence he found surprising in an accomplice of Sun Shulan's.

"I won't hurt you," he said, feeling a need to reassure her. Her skin was flawless, a golden peach color divinely designed to complement the sun-bleached blond of her hair. She was either an angel or the embodiment of a fantasy. He couldn't decide which, but there was an otherworldliness about her, something untamed reflected in the pale crystalline depths of her eyes. He'd never seen eyes like hers. They were more silver than gray.

"No. You won't hurt me," she agreed. "And if you let me go now, I won't hurt you."

So much for innocence, he thought, but he didn't let her go.

"Are you so dangerous?" he asked, one dark eyebrow lifting.

"I can be," she said without hesitation, the gentle lilt of her voice belying her words.

He couldn't resist smiling. "I've been known to be dangerous myself, and I've got at least eighty pounds on you."

"Then I guess I'll just have to take my chances." Sugar was bluffing. She couldn't overpower him, not in her wildest dreams—but a bluff was all she had. Shulan had told her to hold this man, and hold him she would, and make sure he came to no harm. Nothing else had ever been asked in return for the second chance Shulan had given her. She would not fail.

Jackson's smile faded. She was serious. Damn serious. He looked down at her narrow shoulders and her slight build, at the small hand in his, and admitted he knew a couple of ways a one-hundred-and-ten-pound woman could render him helpless, but he doubted if she had anything pleasurably sexual on her mind.

Too bad. He lifted his free hand to touch her hair. Slowly, he ran his fingers through the soft blond mass framing her face and curling around her ears. She wasn't pretty. Pretty was too bland a word to describe her sensual appeal and the contradiction of the fragility of her body when measured against the strength of her conviction. She had no lush curves to entice a man, yet Jackson was enticed—surprisingly, thoroughly.

"What's your name?" he asked.

A dusky rose color blossomed in her cheeks, but her

gaze didn't waver for an instant. "Sugar," she said. "Sugar Caine."

Anyone would have grinned at that, including Jackson, except his gaze had drifted to her lips as she'd spoken. When she'd said Sugar, all he could imagine was how incredibly sweet her mouth would taste.

TWO

She was lovely, all feminine and delicate, and Jackson wanted a taste of her, one kiss, one soft, slow, sweet taste of Sugar Caine.

His grin came then, but it was more at himself than at her name. He'd sworn off wild women a summer ago, and the woman in front of him was wild in ways only a kindred spirit would recognize.

"So, Sugar." His grin turned mocking. "Where did Shulan leave me this time?"

"At the edge of the world." Sugar chose her words carefully. He was no invalid, and she didn't want him getting himself hurt or killed trying to leave her home. There was no escape from Cocorico. Her job wasn't going to be taking care of him; it was going to be making him believe that one irrefutable fact.

"Past this point there be dragons and all that?" he asked, the brief deepening of his smile implying he'd be right at home anyplace there were dragons.

"And all that," she confirmed.

"No," he said, looking around him. "I've been to the edge of the world a couple of times, and this isn't it. Not even close." His gaze came back and settled on her, measuring her, and making her damned uncomfortable.

She glanced away and pretended indifference to his attention. They were physically too close for the kind of scrutiny he was giving her, too close for her peace of mind. She had never been good at hiding her thoughts and emotions, and of all people, she didn't want him seeing her weaknesses—not when wanting someone like him could easily be her greatest weakness. Someone strong and masculine, and so breathtakingly beautiful she could hardly take her eyes off him. Someone to share her life. Someone who could hold her in the night.

She tried to remove her wrist from his hand, but he didn't relent his hold on her.

"Why are you here alone?" he asked.

So much for hiding her weaknesses, she thought, disgusted with herself. Did she look lonely without even trying? Had years of banishment made her utterly transparent?

Well, he wasn't going to get an answer, not even if hell froze over.

"Okay," he said, as if he'd read her mind. She gave him a startled glance. "How about why Shulan brought me to you?"

"To keep you safe," she said, believing honesty was always in her best interest, even if it sometimes took a backseat to silence.

"Then you know about Fang Baolian?"

Her admission consisted of a quick lowering of her lashes, the way she would have admitted to any unsavory bit of knowledge. She knew the Dragon Queen of the South China Sea. Baolian was the bane of her existence.

"She'll kill me if she finds me," he continued, as if he were speaking to a child, explaining the facts of life.

She lifted her eyes and met his gaze squarely. "She won't find you here." Her tone was adamant, her facade one of unadulterated confidence. It had to be, as much for herself as for him.

Jackson looked down at the woman he held using barely half the strength of one hand, once again surprised by the intensity of her conviction. For someone who looked so soft, she had unexpected steel in her backbone.

"What makes you so damn sure?" he asked. Of everything, he wanted to add, but refrained. He knew she'd been bluffing before, about being a danger to him, unless she had the blood of a martial-arts master flowing through her veins. A possibility, he conceded, but for all that steel in her backbone, her body wasn't honed to such a radical degree. He liked to think she wasn't bluffing now, though. The last thing he wanted was for Baolian to find him trapped on an island without an arsenal at his disposal.

"Because she's never found me," Sugar said, and pulled on her wrist. "Now let me go."

Jackson tightened his grip, letting her know he

wasn't ready to release her. "Why would Baolian want you?"

"For the same reason she wants you." She had stopped struggling, but her body remained stiff and resisting.

Without meaning to, he laughed. "I don't think so, Sugar." His gaze dropped to the soft swell of her breasts beneath her white T-shirt. "Not unless Baolian has more eclectic tastes than I thought."

"Not to bed me," she said, color rising in her cheeks.

"So Shulan told you about that part too?"

"Shulan told me what you believe."

"What I believe?" She was full of surprises, Miss Sugar Caine was. He thought back to the last time he'd seen Baolian, stretched out on a bed in a Jakarta luxury hotel, a beguiling smile on her exquisite face, a diaphanous negligee draped across her body, artfully exposing her lush curves.

No. He hadn't mistaken the invitation. Nor had he mistaken Baolian's malice when he'd declined to ensnare himself in her sensual web. The Dragon Queen had made it very clear that from the moment he walked out of the hotel room, he would be living on borrowed time. Her sibilant rantings still echoed in his dreams whenever they edged toward nightmares, which invariably happened when he fell asleep while shackled and chained.

"And what do you believe?" he asked, curious, but not doubting his own conclusions. Baolian had wanted him, and she'd wanted him dead when he hadn't wanted her.

"I believe the truth."

"Which is?"

"Baolian planned to kill you whether you slept with her or not, but she would have enjoyed your death more if she'd first slept with her lover's son. As it stands, she feels cheated. If she finds out you're alive, she'll want to balance the scales before she assigns another assassin to murder you. But this time she won't want sex, she'll want torture."

The word *naive* had been floating across Jackson's mind every time he looked at her. Her face, so open and readable, demanded it, but she'd just shot that theory all to hell. No woman who talked about sex and torture in the same breath, without a qualm, was naive.

"Baolian would torture you?" he asked, though he really didn't want to hear the answer. The woman's skin would bruise too easily. With just his hand he could break her wrist, or her neck. Physically, she was no match for what Baolian could do to her. But with torture, it never came down to the physical. Bodies broke. It wouldn't take that much more pressure to break his arm than it would to break hers.

Spirit was what got people in trouble. Spirit was what wouldn't give way or give up when surrender— even of life itself—was the only way out.

"I'm not planning on giving her the chance," Sugar said, silver fire in her eyes. "If she wants me, she'll have to kill me."

For Jackson, the stakes changed as simply as that.

He bore the mark of Baolian's assassin. He could only imagine what marks Sugar bore.

He released her. "Where am I?"

Sugar immediately moved away from him, giving herself some much-needed distance. "You're in my bedroom," she said, rubbing her wrist and taking another step backward, making sure to keep her gaze level with his. "And you're naked. So, if you don't mind, there are clothes laid out for you on the settee." She gestured toward a rose-colored couch in the corner of the room. "The plumbing is archaic and out back, and if you want to eat, you may meet me in the kitchen after you've dressed."

Before she could make her getaway, her gaze slipped, in total disregard of every mental command she had given her eyes. The lapse only lasted a second, but a second was enough. She hurried out the door with her cheeks burning. Damn the man.

Jackson watched her make her escape, hiding a grin at her curiosity and embarrassment, and reminding himself she was off limits no matter what kind of looks she gave him, or where. He wasn't in the market for a woman, not even one as intriguing as Miss Sugar Caine. He was in the market for a life, his own, the one Baolian had tried to end, the one Shulan had usurped. If it was true what Sugar had said about there only being her and Jen to keep him, then he had as good as won. It took more than a pretty woman full of mysteries and an ancient *wushu* master to hold him captive. Shulan had finally underestimated him.

Without his keeper's presence to distract him, he

took a minute to look around the room. What he saw was almost as otherworldly as the woman. There was no electricity. The soft light he'd seen her by came from a kerosene lantern. There wasn't any glass in the windows. They were covered with slatted wood shutters—jalousies—and nothing else.

He noted the pale aqua sun-washed color of the walls and the worn appearance of the furniture. A blue dresser with a lace cloth draped over its top was pushed up against the wall beneath one of the windows, and like the bedposts it needed paint. The cushion on the wicker chair had been patched. One of the jalousies was hanging askew.

Still, the whole of the room was inviting. Wind chimes captured the night breeze and made music. Outside, the ocean beat upon the shore in a primal rhythm, reminding him of home. There was a sweet smell in the air, of flowers and Sugar, triggering a memory less than two minutes old and of a woman he'd barely met.

"Sugar." He spoke her name softly, liking the sound of it even as he smiled at the absurdity of it. She was wild, all right, both tough and shy, like an animal unused to sharing its territory.

He'd held her close enough and long enough to still feel the imprint of her body against his, to still feel the warmth of her. An image came to him of her lying close to him and of him whispering her sweet name in her ear.

A ripple of sensual awareness started in the nether regions of his body and pooled in his groin—and it was real, no imagining. The wave of desire he felt was physical, seductive, and told him he was alive and well the way nothing else could have.

He poured a glass of water and took a long swallow to cool himself down. His limbs were still weak, and he wondered what the woman would have done if she'd known he was holding on to her as much to keep himself from falling back onto the bed as to keep her from running away.

He didn't wonder long. She would have run. He'd seen it in her eyes. Then she would have come back. He'd seen that, too, right at the end when her gaze had lowered and her expression had softened.

He finished his water and set the glass down. He had work to do. He had to locate Jen. The Chinaman was old, seventy if he was a day, but he was wily, and cunning, and skilled with his swords.

Moonlight slanted through windows and marked his path as he walked silently through the bungalow's rush-matted hallway, tucking his shirttail into the pants she'd left for him. The verandah that lay beyond an arched door led him past green-shuttered windows and scattered pots filled with cacti and flowers. At one end of the covered porch lay the heart of the island enclave, the courtyard.

He stood barefoot on the timeworn wooden decking, looking across the cleared area at a small cottage with a connecting cabana. A light was on inside the cottage, revealing a stove, table, and a rack of cooking utensils—Sugar's kitchen. He'd wondered where it was. The bungalow had only bedrooms in it. At the other end of the verandah was the outhouse, distinguished by its size and the cluster of falling stars cut out of the top of the door. Following his body's demands, he turned toward the outhouse.

The first thing he found inside was the flashlight hanging from the ceiling that bumped him on the head. The plumbing was archaic, as she'd said, but not rustic. When he was finished, he performed his ablutions with the water he found running out of a bamboo pipe attached to the small building. There was also a shelf holding a dish of soap, and a clean towel hanging from a hook by the door.

The wind had picked up, coming in off the water and cooling him through the thin cotton clothes. The drawstring construction of the pants left a lot to be desired, like a fly, but he was past complaining about his wardrobe. The clothes were clean and soft and they smelled good. They were also his favorite color for nighttime—black.

He walked back along the length of the verandah and stood quietly under the thatched roof. Moonlight glittered on the tops of the waves, illuminating the eternal ocean. Behind him, inland, was like a bottomless, formless abyss. He peered into the darkness, trying to discern the landscape. There were trees and another smaller building made of stone, but he couldn't find the horizon.

Fighting an uneasy sensation, he stepped off the verandah. His gaze automatically moved upward, higher and higher, searching for the sky. He found it so far above him, it made his blood run cold.

He was trapped. A towering cliff wall sealed off any

hope of escape inland. A natural stone arch loomed across the top of the cliffs, framing southern stars.

Maybe she was right.

Maybe they were at the edge of the world.

Nothing but the sea sounded at his back, the waves breaking against the rocks tumbled from the cliffs above; nothing but the moon and the stars shone across the black velvet dome of the sky. There was nothing else to be seen or heard, nothing beyond the sea and the sky and the small hold of her home—a fine prison indeed. His only chance might be the water, swimming in a strange ocean at night, and that didn't seem like much of a chance at anything except getting himself killed.

He started to move forward, when the sound of singing and laughter arrested his steps. Silently, he dropped into a crouch. It had not been a woman's laughter, and Jen never laughed.

Sugar halted her actions in the kitchen's cabana, not quite believing her eyes. A half-wrung-out T-shirt dripped water from her hand and onto her bare feet, but she hardly noticed. Her prisoner had disappeared. One instant he'd been standing in the courtyard surveying her home, and in the next he'd melted into the night like a jungle cat on the prowl.

She knew what had spooked him, Henry's drunken rendition of "Island Girl." Truly, it was enough to spook anybody, those wavering high notes hanging on the wind, interspersed with an old man's cackling. Carolina must have put him up to it. Henry never would have expended the effort necessary to get to Cocorico in the dark without some kind of threat inspiring him.

Swearing softly, she dropped the T-shirt back into the washtub and reached behind her to jerk the cord on the generator. When the engine caught, she ran into the kitchen through the side door from the cabana. Old sot that Henry was, he was her friend, and she didn't want to see him come to harm at the hands of the dragon man. She crossed the room, scooting through the narrow space between the table and the north wall, hurrying to reach the switch concealed by a hanging basket full of fruit. Her hand connected with metal, and with a small grunt of effort, she threw the switch.

Painfully bright light flooded the courtyard, freezing everyone in place. Through the west window, Sugar saw Henry swaying on his feet near the clothesline, blinking against the light, but thankfully exposed for what he was, a harmless old man.

Jen was a triangular silhouette of gray next to the icehouse—and he was staring right at her on a line of sight from the cliffs to the interior of the cottage.

A jolt of adrenaline washed into her veins. Whatever she'd expected, it hadn't been to find the Chinaman guarding the entrance to Cocorico and watching her from out of the darkness.

Her prisoner, the dragon man, was harder to spot. She quickly moved around the kitchen table and stationed herself at the front door, ignoring Jen as best she could. Her gaze scanned the courtyard, the beach, and the wilder places spreading away from the cliffs, searching for Jackson. He couldn't have gotten far, but she'd be damned if she could see him.

The reason became clear an instant later when she

was captured from behind and hauled back inside the kitchen.

Her gasp of fear was quickly replaced by one of disbelief when she realized who had her. The dark hair falling over her shoulder and the rock-solid chest at her back didn't leave a doubt in her mind, except she couldn't believe anybody could have moved as fast and as quietly as he had. He must have been almost upon her before she'd even cleared the threshold from the cabana.

"Let go of me, you . . . you—"

"Who's the drunk?" he growled in her ear.

"Henry. He's a friend." She struggled within the viselike circle of his arms, flailing at him. He'd gone too damn far this time.

"Not of mine."

"You don't have any friends," she snapped, anger getting the best of her. She tried to elbow him in the ribs, but he was too quick, shifting his hold but still restraining her. In the next second, though, she fell to the floor, suddenly free.

She looked up at him, ready to lambaste him for his carelessness and threaten him with anything she could dream up—from chains to starvation—if he ever grabbed her again, but her threats would have been redundant. The gleaming blade of Jen's sword lay against his neck, marking him with a thin line of blood.

Her dragon man glared down at her, subjugated by the edge of steel curving toward his throat. His eyes were dark with fury. His fists were clenched at his sides.

"You've made your point, Jen," he muttered between closed teeth. "Now back off before I accidentally kill you." When Jen didn't move, he spoke a stream of Chinese, all of it commanding and angry.

The old man's reply was the silent removal of the weapon, followed by the hushed metallic slither of the sword being sheathed.

Sugar slowly pushed herself to her feet, all of her senses on overdrive. Shulan had brought two warriors and a war to her doorstep, not an invalid in need of care.

"I thought you were here to protect him," she said to Jen, her voice a mixture of admonition and wariness. His rescue had been swift and full of deadly intent; she'd seen the danger in his eyes and felt it in Jackson's reaction.

Shulan had told her many of the details of Jackson's story, but the pirate princess had forgotten to warn her of the old Chinaman's skill. The ancient and fragile Jen was at least as alarming as the dragon man.

"I don't want anybody killed here, accidentally or otherwise," she continued, her gaze taking in both men so there wouldn't be any mistake about whom she was talking to, though she doubted if Jen understood a word she was saying.

She looked at him, as the older and supposedly wiser of the two, but whatever assurances she'd hoped to get weren't going to come from that quarter. He gave her nothing beyond his inscrutable gaze and a short, formal bow before leaving the kitchen. Left without another choice, Sugar let her gaze rise to the man still dominat-

ing the room. Somehow she knew to expect even less
from him.

He was angry, dangerous in the way of all wounded
predators, and he was more than she could handle. She
wasn't prepared to cope with a warrior who only answered to an old man's sword. She had nothing with
which to control him.

Her hand shook as she pulled out one of the
chrome-and-vinyl chairs flanking her wooden table, the
small weakness irritating her further. He shouldn't be
able to unnerve her so easily. Maybe all her longing for
a mate was better left in fantasy, if Jackson Daniels was
the reality.

He wouldn't be staying, of course, but what other
kind of man could she realistically expect to end up on
Cocorico, except one with a violent past and a need to
hide?

Her eyes flicked up once, quickly, then just as
quickly looked away. What she'd seen had not been
encouraging. Dressed, he looked larger than he had
naked, taller and more intimidating—a lot more intimidating.

She should have chosen different clothes for him,
something to counteract the sheer intensity of his presence. The unremitting black of his pants and shirt
heightened the aura of danger around him, and it had
certainly helped him disappear in the courtyard.

"You're bleeding," she said. "Sit down . . .
please." The added politeness was merely that, she told
herself. It was not a plea.

Much to her relief, he did as she asked, lowering

himself into the chair without a complaint. She had no idea what she would have done had he resisted her.

"I'll . . . uh, go get the first-aid supplies," she said, stepping around him and cutting off the floodlights before making her way to the pantry. She wouldn't forget about him wearing black in the night, and she wouldn't let it happen again.

Within moments she was back at his side with her medical kit. She set the large metal box on the table and took from it the antiseptic and a sterile gauze pad. He wasn't hurt too badly, but she didn't want to take a chance on infection setting in.

"That's quite a stash," he said, nodding at the array of pharmaceuticals in the box. "Are you a drug runner or a doctor?"

"I've got an out-of-date Red Cross card," she said, "and that's almost as good as a medical license out here."

"Out where?"

"Here," she said, not missing his crude attempt to get information from her. He was still angry. She could tell by the tension in his body and the barely perceptible twitching of the muscles in his jaw. But he was controlling his emotions—thank God—trying to come down off the inevitable adrenaline rush of finding a sword ready to cut his throat.

She lifted the antiseptic-soaked pad to clean his wound, but her hand paused near his shoulder, heeding an intuitive warning: Touching the dragon man was a risky thing to do.

The only times they'd had contact, he'd grabbed

her, taken her by surprise. There had been no premeditation on her part, and to the best of her ability, she had not touched him back. The choice was lost to her now.

Chiding herself for foolishness, she used her free hand to smooth his hair behind his ear—and immediately knew her fears had not been foolish.

The warmth of his skin unsettled her, making her aware of the pure animal aliveness of him. Equally startling was the texture of his hair. She would not have guessed it to be so sinfully soft and sensuous, so at odds with the hard strength of his body. The straight dark strands slid through her fingers and drifted across her palm as she moved them aside to expose his throat. With absentminded care, she trailed the pads of her fingers along the back of his neck, feeling the heat and vulnerability of his nape, and the subtle shift he made to increase their contact.

He wasn't dangerous to touch. He was heaven, strong and warm, sensual and responsive, his body so wonderfully different from hers.

The rising of his lashes captured her attention and drew her thoughts away from his silken hair. She lowered her eyes to meet his—and was trapped by the green fire of his knowing gaze. Mortified, she pulled her hand away, letting his hair return to his back and slide to his waist.

To his credit, he didn't give her one of his wry smiles. He didn't tease her. She almost wished he had, anything to break the embarrassment engulfing her.

"This is going to sting," she said, forcing the few words out and using the most clinical voice she could manage with a full-blown blush coursing across her cheeks. She'd been fondling the man.

He said nothing, only glanced away after a reflective perusal of her eyes. When she went on to clean his wound, he didn't flinch. Not so much as a flicker of discomfort showed on his face, though she knew from experience that the antiseptic stung like the dickens. She finished tending him, fighting twinges of guilt as she added another bandage to match the one on his shoulder. He wasn't supposed to have gotten hurt while under her care. Something had to be done with him, before anything else happened.

"I don't want you to touch me again," she said. That sounded good, real good, and would certainly help with her overawareness of him. She smoothed a strip of first-aid tape into place. "If you'll keep your hands to yourself, I'm sure Jen will do the same with his swords. You're safe while you're here, so there's no need to go around attacking people."

"I wasn't attacking you," he said, sounding at least as irritated with himself as she was with herself. "I was protecting you."

She gave him an incredulous look. "From Henry?"

"From a stranger. You said there was no one else here. Only you, and me, and Jen." He turned his head to meet her gaze. "Don't lie to me, Sugar," he warned. "I've got damn few facts to work with to keep myself alive."

She'd never been called a liar. It was an utterly novel and not very pleasant experience.

"When we were in the bungalow," she said, "there

were only three people here. I'm not sure why Henry came back tonight, but I asked him not to return until morning."

"Why?"

"In case you still hadn't come around." She crossed the first piece of tape with another.

"What would you have done with me, if I hadn't?"

"I would have gotten you better medical care."

He shot her a hard look. "In other words, if I die, I can leave."

She just stared at him, appalled at the conclusion he'd drawn. "You were brought here so you would be safe. I am supposed to take care of you. I can take of you," she told him, feeling far more than her pride was at stake. "You aren't in danger. I swear."

A short bark of laughter escaped him, the sound as good as calling her a liar again.

"I am not lying to you," she said. "Shulan's only concern is for your welfare."

In answer, he lifted one winged eyebrow in a clear show of derision. "If you believe that, then I obviously know your friends a hell of a lot better than you know .mine."

Sugar felt just enough contrition for her earlier words to offer him an apology. The man had been wounded and captured. Antagonizing him would get her nowhere. Insulting him was unnecessary and mean. "I'm sorry. I'm sure you have lots of friends, some-where."

His answer to her apology was more laughter and sarcasm. "My, my, you are sweet, aren't you?"

"Not really," she said, feeling foolish. The man didn't need her sympathy, and she'd do well to remember it.

"No?"

"No." She was emphatic.

"Ah, then you're just in it for the money."

She gave him a wary look. "What money?"

"The ransom Shulan wants for dragging me off that beach before her mother's lackey dog could get another shot at me.

"She better be asking for a bundle," he went on. "I would guess Baolian's maternal instincts will be running on empty if she ever finds out what her little girl has gone and done. The Dragon Queen wanted me dead. She's not going to be happy to find out I survived her ambush, and she isn't going to be happy with the person who helped me, blood relative or not."

"You've got it all wrong," Sugar said, turning toward the table to repack her medical kit. "Shulan is saving you for the same reason her mother wants you killed, because you are Sun Yi's son. There is no ransom."

"Right," he drawled, clearly calling her a liar yet again. "And you don't have the kind of legs men dream about in their sleep." He rose from the chair and walked over to the window overlooking land's end, leaving her speechless behind him. "He's still out there, wandering around."

"Jen or—or Henry?" she asked, wanting to prove to him he hadn't stunned her senseless with his matter-of-fact summation.

"Henry." He laughed softly. "Jen doesn't wander, physically or mentally. That's what makes him such a good watchdog. He's got the tenacity and focus of a heat-seeking missile. Which is great, unless you're the damn target."

He swore, a rude word, and turned to face her, dragging his hands back through his hair. He stood staring at her, his gaze raking her from head to foot, his expression a mixture of resentment and fascination.

"I don't know where she found you, but Shulan chose you well. So damn well, it makes me wonder if the drugs she used gave her access to my fantasies . . . because you are it, lady. But that's not enough to keep me on this rock."

If he expected an answer from her, he was going to be sorely disappointed. She didn't have anything to say to such an outrageous statement—or so she thought. The longer he stood there staring at her, looking like he wanted to either beat her or eat her, the more inclined she became to speak.

"You're w-wrong again," she stammered. "Shulan isn't asking for a ransom, and she knows better than to ask anything like what you're suggesting of me."

"Sex is the oldest lure on the face of the earth." He took a step forward.

"Not on my corner of it," she said, inadvertently stepping back.

His half smile and the satisfaction darkening his eyes alerted her to what she'd done. She cursed silently. She couldn't afford to let him have the upper hand, and when he took his next step forward, she held her ground.

"There are a couple of things you need to know before I leave you to eat your dinner," she said, stiffening her backbone in the face of his slow, predatory approach.

"Such as?" He cocked one brow in question.

"You're nine miles from the nearest inhabited landfall. Off the leeward point of the island is a deep ocean trough that's called Shark Alley for a reason, and you're bleeding. I wouldn't be going for any midnight swims if I were you."

Her piece said, she turned and walked out the door, barely clearing the porch before a stream of virulent curses burst from the kitchen.

THREE

Jackson stood on a jetty of rocks in the fading moonlight, watching the sea ply its trade. Sounds of the island came from behind him, filling the lull between waves with the chirping of crickets and the peeping of tree frogs. The faintest brightening on the rim of the arch told him dawn was nearly at hand.

He'd eaten the meal she'd laid out for him of rice, beans, and fruit, and he'd cleaned up as best he could without knowing where everything went. Most of all he'd enjoyed the freedom of being alone, of eating without being watched, of being able to move around without anyone following him. Even the old Chinaman had let him be.

If anything that night, he was the watcher. Henry, the drunk, had curled up under a blanket in the cabana off the kitchen, too far gone to make questioning him anything other than a lesson in futility. All Jackson had learned was of Henry's penchant for a lovely but heartlessly cruel woman named Carolina. Jen was asleep on a pallet in the icehouse, having commandeered that dilapidated building for himself, and Sugar Caine was in the bedroom next to the one she'd given him in the green-shuttered bungalow, tossing and turning. Her light had come on numerous times in the night, bare strips of illumination leaking through the jalousies, telling him of her restlessness.

He knew he was the cause. The way she'd touched him while tending his wound had told him more about her life and her needs than anything she'd said. There had been tenderness in her caress, in the softness of her fingers on his shoulder, in the gentle exploration she'd made of the back of his neck; tenderness and a reverence that had made him wonder how long she'd been alone. She'd let herself linger over the moving aside of his hair, playing with the length of it and sighing so quietly, he would have missed the revealing sign except for the rise and fall of her small breasts. The slight movement had fascinated him, tantalizing in all its possibilities. When he'd lifted his gaze to meet hers, he'd seen a reflection of his own desire in the soft gray depths of her eyes.

Strange, beautiful woman-child. What could she have done to Baolian?

He raised his head and turned toward the bungalow where she slept. Fireflies flitted through the under-growth encroaching on the courtyard and through the numerous pots of flora on the porch. A stand of bamboo canopied the rickety stairs leading from the bungalow to the beach, where coconut palms sighed with the wind, their fronds swaying in the cool currents of air.

Paradise or hell? He still didn't know, except Sugar Caine looked more like an angel than a demon, and she fought the same devil he did.

Her light came on again, and his pulse quickened, surprising him. What had Shulan done by bringing him here?

Sugar slipped into her sandals and doused the lantern. Her days started early no matter how short the night had been. Today would be no exception. Henry wouldn't stay drunk forever, and she wanted him off the island before he got too sober, before Jackson Daniels cornered him and started asking questions. What made Henry the perfect courier and liaison was his guilelessness and general state of confusion, not his discretion. She'd shared a few bottles of rum with the old man, and they both had a tendency to get maudlin as hell in their cups. Even only half-coherent, Henry might tell the dragon man more about her than she wanted him to know.

She closed the bungalow door behind her and stood for a moment, buttoning her jacket. The northeast trade wind had blown through the night, keeping Cocorico cool and carrying the mists out over the ocean. The sun would come early this morning.

Finishing the last button, she started down the stairs to the beach. It was more ritual than necessity to walk the headlands, but she wanted to check the surrounding seas and assure herself there wouldn't be any unexpected arrivals. Sometimes unwary sailors laid anchor off the island, though a stop in any nearby port would have warned them away. Shark Alley was real and marked on the maps, making Cocorico a poor choice for diving.

Beach morningglories climbed over the rocks, spreading across the sand at the bottom of the stairs and all along the base of the cliffs. She checked the windward side of the island first, knowing it was the least likely place for a stranger to anchor, in the buffeting winds that came off the Atlantic. For a friend, though, it was the only choice, in the hidden cove carved out of the limestone on the other side of the arch.

When she saw no mast or rigging silhouetted against the pale sky, she made her way down the rocks to the beach. Cocorico was a crescent-shaped curve of land, about three hundred yards long. As on the windward side, the leeward boundary of the bay was demarcated by a jetty of rocks carved from the cliffs above.

She picked her way across the tide pools and over the ragged-edged boulders, making for the farthest point of land, and was almost upon him before she realized it. She stopped suddenly, the soft splash of her last step fading into the rhythmic pounding of the surf.

He'd seen her. She knew it, or she would have turned and tried to slip away.

He stood above her, at the top of the jetty with his arms at his sides, his legs spread and braced. The dawn wind molded his clothes to him, the thin cotton revealing the strength of firm flanks and a broad chest.

Wind lifted his hair and sent it rippling like a dark veil down the side of his body. He was the vision of a warrior, an image of power as constant as the sea. In the last shadows of the night, he took her breath away.

"I've been watching the sharks," he said, his voice carrying above the sound of the waves.

She nodded, not trusting herself to speak. She didn't want him here, invading her sanctuary and wrecking her hard-won peace, bringing violence and longing back into her life. She had run from violence once and escaped it. The longing she'd subdued and ignored, sublimated it in order to survive alone.

But he'd lain in her bed, filling it with his body, so much larger than her own, claiming it with his scent and presence. She'd felt longing again, a need to be held, a desire to feel a man's mouth on hers, to know the caress of his hands.

Was it so wrong to want what she couldn't have? Or was it merely the pain of the wanting that made it foolish, a masochist's idyll?

And if she was going to be tempted, why couldn't the temptation be easier to resist? She remembered there being hundreds, if not thousands, millions, of average-looking men in the world, and she'd be the first to admit they had their appeal. A man like Jackson Daniels was overkill in the temptation department. His body was a masterwork of form and curve and sentient masculinity that any woman would want to touch and explore. He would have tempted a saint, and she was no saint.

"Come," he said. "There's a ship."

Nothing else he could have said would have impelled her to accept the hand he offered. Not when she'd spent the whole night devising ways to keep her distance, to build barriers between them so there would be less danger of him making an impression on a heart that she knew was desperately impressionable.

His fingers closed around hers, and he pulled her up with startling ease, positioning her in front of him. Physically, she was no match for him; she was a complement. He had the strength of power, she had the strength to endure. He was tawny-skinned and dark-haired. Everything about her was fair, even the shade of her inevitable tan. His body was large, angles and planes of muscle layered over a broad-shouldered frame. She was slender, her muscles hidden beneath softer curves.

He was a man, she a woman. Male and female.

"Off the point," he said, pointing to where a cargo boat cut through the waves about a mile offshore.

"You never would have made it." She tried to ignore how close she was to him, close enough to feel the warmth of his body as they balanced on the rough stones.

"I'm a pretty good swimmer," he said with a shrug, not taking his eyes off the boat.

Even if he had made it, she doubted if the captain of the *Mary Sue* would have done anything except shoot him, the same thing a captain would do to any man, woman, beast, or fish that came up out of the ocean in the middle of the night and tried to board his boat.

A quick wisp of sound and shadow passed through the air above them, then another, and another. She felt his hand curve around her upper arm as more of the small creatures filled the sky, darting and weaving a path home before the sun rose.

He moved closer to her, making her wonder how deep his protective instincts ran. The whole of Cocorico was a sanctuary, a place where she needed no protection, a place to which he'd been brought to be protected, and yet twice he'd put himself between her and a perceived harm. She only hoped he would let her do the same for him while he was there.

"You have a lot of bats in paradise, Miss Caine," he said, taking the last step necessary to bring his chest against her back. The warmth of him seeped through her jacket and T-shirt, and she had to fight the urge to lean into him.

"The red bats started arriving last week," she said, "migrating south, bringing the island back up to three confirmed species. A few months ago I found a small carcass on the beach that looked like a Pallas's long-tongued bat. But there wasn't enough left of it to positively identify." She knew she sounded like an educational tape on West Indian flying mammals, but it was hard to sound natural when she was holding her breath to keep from letting out the sigh building in her throat.

The cloud of tiny animals was passing them by. She hadn't realized how tense he'd been until he relaxed his hold on her and stepped back to his original position.

"Don't you like bats?" she asked, looking at him to better gauge his answer. Maybe he'd gotten close to her because he'd felt threatened. It wouldn't hurt for her to know his weaknesses. Not so she could exploit them, but so she could ease as much of the stress out of his life as possible. He still had some healing to do.

"I like them fine," he replied. "But I've never met a woman who did."

As far as she could see, he was telling the truth. He'd been protecting her again, not looking for protection for himself.

"It took me a while to learn to like them," she said, a confession she'd only made to Carolina. "I grew up in the islands, so I was used to bats. I just wasn't used to having so many of them live so close."

"And now?"

"And now I figure God made the bats, even the strange ones, just like She made all the cute things like puppies and ladybugs, and all the elegant things like jaguars and Arabian horses."

"She?" he repeated in a tone that made a grin twitch at the corners of her mouth.

"Do you have a problem with that, Mr. Daniels?" she asked with a guileless glance in his direction.

"Not me." Jackson couldn't believe his luck, or rather the lack thereof. Not only had he been stranded on an island with his unattainable sexual fantasy, she was a feminist. There was a lesson to be learned from that, he was sure. Maybe it was penance for past deeds, though he'd be damned if he could think of a woman he needed to do penance for. He recalled a few tearful farewells, but that was part of living. Nobody got through life without having her—or his—heart broken, without crying for somebody who wasn't coming back.

He looked down at the woman sharing the jetty and

the moonlight with him, and he wondered whom she cried for. He wondered who cried because she wasn't coming back, and suddenly he was angry again.

"Don't you ever want to leave this place?" he asked, his voice harsher than he'd meant it to be.

The teasing smile faded from her lips, and he felt like a first-class bastard. She couldn't have much in her life, and he'd just stolen her smile.

She shouldn't let herself be so vulnerable.

"Well, I do," he answered when she didn't.

"You can't leave the island," she said, turning away from him. "There's no way off, and if you try to find a way, or make a way, you're only going to get yourself hurt."

"What about you?" he asked. "What's going to hurt you? Going to jail for aiding and abetting a criminal? A kidnapping charge? Or doesn't it bother you that what you're doing is wrong?"

Sugar blanched at his words. She'd let her guard down, allowed herself to pretend they were two normal people, and now she was paying the price of feeling betrayed when anyone in his situation would be a fool not to use her emotions against her.

Though wide of a legal mark, his accusations laid open a truth she hadn't fully acknowledged: However altruistic she and Shulan considered their actions, he saw only that he'd been captured and detained. But he was wrong.

"You're damned ungrateful for a person who could have been dead by now," she said, giving him her version of the situation.

He looked down at her again and laughed, a self-deprecating sound that grew until she was thoroughly humiliated.

"It's true," she said.

"You call this living?" he replied, gesturing around himself. "Being holed up on an island full of bats and surrounded by sharks?" The look he gave her definitely included her in the description.

"I'm not a bat or a shark."

"No? Then what are you, Sugar Caine? A beautiful woman with a strange name who lives all alone in paradise doing God knows what with her days? Or are you Shulan's warden, the keeper of her private penitentiary?"

"This isn't a penitentiary," she said, trying to maintain her equanimity and failing miserably. "It's my home, and for the record, I keep damn busy with my days. I have a job."

"A job?" he asked, not sounding for a second as if he believed her.

"Yes." She didn't have much, but she did have work to support herself. She wasn't a charity case living off her father, or Shulan.

He was silent for a long moment, looking down at her with one eyebrow raised in doubt.

"Well?" he finally asked, his question clear.

"I garden," she said. "I'm a gardener."

The silence lengthened uncomfortably again, until he broke it with a snide remark.

"A hell of a job, I'm sure," he said, then climbed down the rocks toward the beach.

Sugar turned her gaze toward the sea, refusing to feel the hurt he'd inflicted with his casual dismissal of the one thing she had to keep her going.

The *Mary Sue* slipped past the point, on its way to Kingstown. No doubt it carried some supplies destined for Cocorico—she was due to restock both her larder and her laboratory, such as it was—but no regularly scheduled ferries stopped at Cocorico. Henry was the only one who brought her supplies and took out her shipments, the small packages of seeds she harvested from the rare and endangered tropical plants she cultivated in her gardens. Once a month he also brought Carolina to stay for a few days. More rarely, her father deserted his medical practice for a day or two to visit, and even more rarely, her mother. A few botanists, ethnobotanists, and research associates had come and gone over the years. She was sure more would come, and she was just as sure that they all would leave.

Nobody stayed. Nobody.

Jackson made it all the way to the beach stairs before guilt got the better of him. He'd behaved like a jerk. He should go back and apologize, but he could think of few things stupider than for a captive to apologize to his captor. Whether she spent her days gardening or not, she was still the one keeping him on this rock in the middle of nowhere. There had to be a way off, and until she revealed it to him, she was the enemy, she and Jen.

That still left the drunk, Henry.

The thought no sooner formed than it catapulted

him into action. He lengthened his stride and took the stairs two at a time all the way to the top. The old man had had all night to sleep off his rum. It was time to question him again. He only had to make sure he didn't alert Jen. Without a weapon, he was at the Chinaman's mercy.

Sugar wiped at a stubborn tear with the back of her hand, turning just in time to see Jackson clear the top step and break into a run for the kitchen cottage.

"Damn," she muttered, and took off after him, her tears forgotten in the burst of panic she felt. She knew what he was up to. Henry.

Minutes later she cleared the cabana threshold and came to a skidding stop. It was empty. The blanket she'd given Henry was wadded up into a ball on a caned chair. The rucksack he always kept with him wasn't anywhere in sight.

The smell of coffee brought her head around toward the kitchen, the aroma making her swear under her breath. Jackson hadn't had time to make coffee. He hadn't been that far ahead of her. Henry must have awakened and made the coffee, and the two of them were probably in the kitchen talking up a storm. The old sailor was as garrulous as he was guileless.

Her body tense, she strode into the kitchen, ready to break up the party. There was no party, though. There was only one dragon man holding a cup of steaming brew, staring out the window at the sea with his back to the rest of the room.

"You lied to me again," he said, not bothering to turn around.

She scanned the kitchen on her way to check the pantry. Henry had a sweet tooth. More than once she'd found him rustling through her grocery supplies, looking for candy or cane.

The small room was empty.

"He's gone," Jackson said as she crossed behind him, heading for the porch.

"Don't bother," Jackson called after her. "I've already checked the whole damn place, and all I found was Jen."

She looked anyway, then came back to stand in the doorway.

"He could be wandering around outside," she said. "Henry likes to wander."

"No. Jen got rid of him."

A shiver of fear rippled down her spine. "What do you mean?"

"I mean everybody here seems to know how to leave except me." He turned and leveled her with an angry gaze. "I've been all over this place tonight. It's like a damn fortress with those cliffs, and I haven't seen so much as a raft for transportation. How did Henry get away? Fly? Swim? Beam up?"

She wasn't going to answer his question. There was only one way out of Cocorico, and Jen had made his camp in the icehouse that concealed the old pirate's door.

Jackson swore at her silence and turned back toward the window. She walked over to the stove and poured herself a cup of the still-hot coffee. The fragrant steam tickled her nose as she took her first sip. There were few luxuries in her life. Jamaican Blue Mountain coffee was one of them.

She looked up at him over the rim of her mug. He hadn't moved from in front of the window. Within the quarter-paned glass—it was the only window that still had glass—the sun was climbing up into the arch, rimming it with brilliant light.

"God, you don't even have a phone or a radio." He shook his head in disgust, and his hair swayed in a long sinuous line from his shoulders to his hips, ebony silk against the black cotton shirt. "There are no clothes in the laundry except yours, no clothes in your bedroom except yours. You have one rain slicker hanging in the cabana and one toothbrush in a cup by the sink. As far as I can tell, you don't get mail or pay bills. You don't have a canceled check or an invoice anywhere in the house."

"You have no right to go through my things," she said.

He glanced at her over his shoulder. "Yeah, well, we're all pretty damn short of rights around here."

It was a useless point to argue, Sugar knew. He was going to do as he pleased, and the only way she could stop him was to call on Jen. Considering the Chinaman's methods, she'd rather deal with Jackson's searches than have to doctor him up again. The only things she had to hide were her feelings and the way out of Cocorico.

"You do have plants, though," he admitted with a

sigh. "Hundreds of them. Thousands. Probably millions." He faced her fully, the barest trace of contrition showing in the curve of his mouth. "I saw your potting room, or whatever you call it, off the cabana. I'm sorry about what I said out on the beach."

She could have thrown his apology back in his face, the way he'd done with hers. Vindictiveness wasn't part of her nature, though, and she didn't want another war on her hands. It was bad enough having him and Jen at each other's throats.

"I have close to forty endangered species I'm cultivating at any one time. All the other plants are indigenous, or planted for pleasure or eating."

"It's still a lot of plants." The faintest grin touched his lips again. "It's like living in an out-of-control greenhouse."

He was miserable. She knew it, but she didn't know what to do about it. He'd spent his first day on Cocorico unconscious, and his first night prowling the beach alone, looking for a way off that wasn't there. She knew what it felt like to be trapped. But freedom had been her trap and Cocorico her sanctuary.

"You won't be here very long," she said, hoping to encourage him. "Three weeks on the outside."

"Then what?" He quirked one eyebrow in an expression she found uniquely his, a combination of irony and ingenuousness that made him seem both young and old.

"Then Shulan comes back," she said, watching the dawn light spill through the window behind him, revealing the details of his face.

"I'd rather be gone before she gets here."

Sunshine gilded the line of his jaw and the angle of his cheekbone. As light washed into his eyes, turning the shadowy forest color into a vibrant emerald green, something in her chest constricted.

Not her heart, she told herself even as she covered the left side of her rib cage with her hand to ease the strange sensation. The ache was probably nothing more than a wayward emotion caused by having him at Cocorico. She couldn't remember the last time she had shared a sunrise. That novelty alone was enough to drag up all sorts of baggage, whether he knew they were sharing the moment or not.

He would be gone soon, and that was for the best. He wasn't very old. He had the rest of his life to live, somewhere else.

"I can't let you go."

He gave her a reluctant nod, as if he understood her position, and took a swallow of coffee. For a moment she thought their conversation was over, but then he spoke.

"I have a brother, an older brother," he said. "His name is Cooper. He raised me, and I'm pretty sure he thinks I'm dead. He was with me when I got shot, guarding my back while I was guarding his. He's got to be going through hell, blaming himself for what happened."

Guilt assailed her and forced her eyes to shift away from his. She hadn't thought about his family, other than Shulan.

"You have to let me go, Sugar. You can't keep me here against my will."

"What makes you think I'm not here against mine?" she asked, making sure to give the question no betraying inflection.

Despite her effort, his gaze sharpened and hope lit the depths of his eyes. "Then you could leave with me," he said softly, urgently.

No, she couldn't. She set her coffee cup down on the counter and walked over to the kitchen cabana door. On the threshold, she paused. She knew what else she had to say, yet she hesitated, knowing her words would give away more of herself than she wanted to reveal.

Still, she had to do it.

She looked in his direction, but couldn't quite meet his eyes. She didn't want to watch his hopes dim, and the words were hard enough to say without him looking inside her and finding the truth of her loneliness.

"If I could leave the island and have a life to live, I would," she said. "But I can't, ever, and for now, neither can you."

FOUR

Two days later Sugar wasn't sure she was going to survive having Jackson Daniels dropped on her doorstep. He was the ultimate invasion of privacy, an immovable wall and an unstoppable force all rolled into one.

Sweating and swearing under the midday sun, she laid another bead of caulk down the last glass window on the place. She lived in an ever-changing, never-ending tableau of the handyman's dream. On Cocorico, if it was metal, it rusted; if it was wood, it warped; if it was paint, it peeled; and if it was a roof, it leaked.

The caulk stopped running, and she set her jaw, squeezing harder on the trigger of the caulking gun. The upkeep of the cottage and the bungalow was too much for one person, especially if that person was more conversant with *Bactris gasipaes palmae* than a hammer and saw. Adding the baby-sitting of other people's long-lost, half-wild half brothers didn't make her job any easier.

After Jackson's first night on the island, Jen had found a cache of supplies in a hollow of limestone above the high-tide mark. Sugar had put everything back in the pantry and had talked again with her "guest" about Shark Alley and the folly of leaving. The next day Jen had discovered a partially completed raft hidden in the shrubs and undergrowth at the base of the cliffs. The two of them had spent most of the morning dismantling the rough craft. She hated to think of what Jackson might come up with next.

She finished the seam with the last dollop of caulk and lifted her head to survey her work. It looked like hell. Fortunately, a certain degree of shabbiness could be interpreted as tropical ambience. People paid thousands of dollars for tropical ambience. She probably ought to quit fooling with Cocorico's before she wore herself out. She reached for the glass of lemonade she'd put in the window's flower box, silently admitting that Henry wasn't the only person who'd gotten the gumption sucked out of him by the Caribbean sun.

Proving her point again, Jackson Daniels chose that moment to step onto the bungalow's verandah. She took one look at him walking over to gaze at the ocean, leaning with his hands on the porch rail, and her heart sank.

"Damn it all," she muttered under her breath, setting her lemonade back in the geraniums. He'd found the box of clothes she'd put in his room, a box she should have had the sense to go through before giving him carte blanche.

On the front of the T-shirt he'd chosen to wear, the

words *I get my Sugar Caine in the British Windwards* were silk-screened in letters two inches high. She couldn't read it at that distance, but she didn't need to be able to read it. The white shirt was distinctive, with both sleeves ripped out, the bottom cut off, and the letters painted in bright aqua over a map of the islands. The darn thing was supposed to have ended up in the ragbag years ago, when her father had run off the boy who'd had the gall to make it.

"Ah, hell." She wasn't cut out for subterfuge. Shulan should have known better than to bring him to her. All her hemming and hawing about his location had been a waste of breath, because he was standing there with the information plastered across his chest.

And he knew it. He had to know it.

She lifted her hand to shade her eyes, watching him from across the courtyard. The striped shadows of the verandah's thatched roof veiled his face and hid his expression, but she thought she detected an easiness in his stance that hadn't been there before. She'd left him in a fit of temper—again—when she'd gotten up a few hours before dawn to check on, and if necessary curtail, his nighttime activities. If his mood had improved at all, it had to be because he'd read the T-shirt and realized its significance.

He slowly straightened from the rail, and just as slowly, her gaze shifted from his face, drifting down the silky length of his hair, past the bare strip of his abdomen, and over his hips, where the drawstring pants hung only by the grace of God.

Lord, he was beautiful—barefoot and alluring, this

son of a pirate. His movements were fluid and controlled, like Jen's, but with the added strength of youth and the added distraction of lean, hard muscle layered over a quintessentially masculine body.

Beautiful men were not a rare commodity in the Caribbean. In years gone by, Sugar had seen her share of hard, bronzed chests, rock-solid abs, and rakish smiles, but Jackson Daniels was different. He had an aura of power about him, purposeful, inherently regal, and magnetic, like a lodestone. It was what made him dangerous. It was also what made him fascinating.

She lowered her hand and unconsciously balled it into a fist. Shulan had asked for too much by bringing him here. Someone had to be looking for him, some woman who missed him in the night. Some woman who ached for wondering what had become of him. He must have been loved—and with that face, probably too many times for his own good.

Her expression turning grim, she picked up the lemonade glass and headed toward the cabana. A woman *was* looking for him, she reminded herself, a woman with murder, not love, on her mind. Her job was to protect him from Baolian, care for him, and let him go. Nothing more.

Leaning against the verandah railing, Jackson looked out to sea, following a wave in from open water until it broke upon the shore. He followed the next, and the next, and the next, discerning the tide, the currents, and the undertow. He watched the last wave turn to foam and froth before it sank into the sand.

The Windward Islands. He was in the Caribbean. The realization had shocked him. Whatever Shulan was up to, she sure as hell was going out of her way to get it. There were a thousand islands in the South China Sea and the South Pacific. She could have had her pick of them rather than come so far from her home territory. Unless that had been the point, to get away, far away from Fang Baolian and her army of cutthroats and spies.

He had a lot of questions, and there wasn't anyone to stop him from getting the answers out of the island woman. Except Jen.

He gingerly touched the healing cut on the side of his neck. The Chinaman was a problem, but not an insurmountable one if Sugar became Jackson's ally instead of the old man's. Shulan wouldn't have miscalculated Sugar's appeal to him. She would have expected it, used it, depended on it to keep him where she wanted him to be. Sugar might be too naive to believe anyone bartered sex, but he didn't have a doubt, and he'd seen the way she looked at him. Shulan would have betted on that too. It was time for him to work a little harder at attracting Miss Sugar Caine, instead of being so damn good at arguing with her and scaring her off.

A self-deprecating smile curved his lips. That's what had gotten him into this mess in the first place, trying to lure a woman into a trap. Baolian had been intrigued by the bait, but when he hadn't delivered the goods, namely himself, she'd gotten nasty.

He didn't think that was going to be a problem with

Sugar. If his life depended on it, he would gladly sacrifice whatever was left of his virtue in Sugar's bed, on her rickety kitchen table, on her beach. She could pick the place, and the time, and the position.

Once again, though, given the way his luck had been running, he doubted if anything as desirable as sex with Sugar was going to get him off the island.

He looked up from the ocean and over his shoulder at the limestone cliffs towering at his back. In daylight he'd seen the beauty of her home, and the absoluteness of its isolation. They were in a rock bowl resting on its side, facing north, offered up to the sun and the sea with the arch as its handle. Inside the bowl was a lush paradise of greenery and trees fed by a stream that fell in four tiers from openings in the cliff wall. The rock was slick with vegetation and moisture in some places, friable in others. Climbing out to find whatever was on the other side of the cliffs would have to be a last resort, one step above swimming through the sharks and the riptide.

The Caribbean hideaway was a true Garden of Eden, untouched, full of life's ripeness, and the wildest creature in the garden was Sugar Caine. He lowered his gaze to the sun-drenched courtyard, looking for his prey, a woman with the face of a young angel and eyes the color of a dove's wings.

Sugar stepped out of the cabana, carrying a basket over one arm. The polite thing to do would be to go over and say good morning to her guest and let him know she would have his breakfast ready in a few minutes. Instead, she was heading toward her melon patch and her fruit trees, determined to avoid the polite thing and Jackson Daniels for as long as possible.

She was halfway to the orchard when her common sense sent her a news flash: ignoring Jackson wasn't the best way to control him. She'd been going about everything all wrong. What she needed to do was damnably clear—spend more time trying to entertain him and keep him busy so that he'd have less time for his doomed escape plans. So that he'd be less likely to get himself killed while under her care.

With a muttered curse, she pivoted on her heel. She continued cursing all the way across the courtyard, stopping only when she was close enough that he might hear.

"Good morning," she hollered out, stepping up onto the verandah, a brightly false smile plastered to her face.

"Good morning," he said, his voice gravelly from sleep and impossibly seductive. He turned to face her, running a hand back through his hair, and the bottom fell out of Sugar's heart.

The shirt was an unmitigated disaster, revealing not only his location in the Windwards, but enough bared abdomen to spark a riot of memories. Dragon's wings unfurled from beneath the ragged edge of the T-shirt, blue and green on tawny skin, the creature's musculature rippling with the movement of the man.

Her gaze followed the curve of the dragon's tail to Jackson's navel and the line of soft dark hair arrowing beneath his pants. The first time she'd seen so much of him there had been no pants, no small black bow of a drawstring underneath his navel, as if he were a gift of erotica from the gods.

He'd already been unwrapped.

A blush heated up her cheeks. She would never forgive Shulan for bringing him here. The pirate princess must have known he wasn't in need of her limited nursing skills. She must have known Sugar was going to have to deal with him all day long, every day, and into the night, and . . .

"There's coffee in the kitchen," she said abruptly, cutting off her thoughts before they got any worse. "I was just going out to the gardens." What she had to say next was easily the worst idea she'd had in months, but she still thought it was better than the alternative. "You could . . . uh, grab a cup and come along if you like."

The invitation was painfully forced and insincere, but Jackson didn't care. He was just grateful, and surprised, to have gotten it at all.

"Sure. That sounds great."

"Great," she said, giving him another patently false smile.

He almost laughed, but held it back. She didn't need to know he could see through her. Better to let her play this new game her way.

He fell in step beside her, and between the two of them, they managed enough awkward conversation to get them to the kitchen.

"Pretty hot today."

"It's unusual for this time of year."

"Does it rain every day?"

"Every afternoon," she confirmed.

The conversation died its first death as quickly as that. He should have known the weather wouldn't get him very far. Caribbean meteorology was blandly perfect, give or take a hurricane or two. After a few yards in silence, he tried another subject.

"Have you heard from Henry?"

The look she gave him was clearly the only reply he was going to get.

"Thanks for the toothbrush and all the other supplies," he said, trying a new tack.

"You're welcome."

"And the clothes," he added, glancing down to catch her reaction.

It was worth the effort.

The color in her cheeks heightened, though she stared doggedly ahead. "I should have looked through the box."

"Don't worry about it. It's not that much information."

"Right," she said dryly, leading the way up the cottage steps. "It's just a map, that's all."

"I was more interested in the message."

"Oh." Her blush deepened.

He followed her into the kitchen, his gaze drifting down the length of her legs. Lord, she was sweet.

"So who got you?" he asked.

She literally tripped over the question, catching herself with a hand on the table before she could fall.

"No one got me," she said with acerbity, taking a

cup out of the tall cabinet next to the stove. She kept her eyes downcast while she filled the cup with coffee.

"Okay," he said slowly. "So who thinks he got you?"

The coffeepot rattled as she set it back on the stove. Sugar snatched her hand away and busied herself with the totally unnecessary act of folding a kitchen towel. She'd known this was a bad idea, a damn bad idea, and she'd be damned if she entertained him with her deep dark secrets.

"You ask a lot of questions." She put the towel on the counter and picked up her basket to leave.

"And you tell me everything except what I want to know," he said. "What's the problem, Sugar? Do you have something to hide? What is it you're so afraid of me finding out?"

His accusation hit a nerve dead on and stopped her in her tracks. She'd tried being nice, but they had hardly managed five minutes of civility before they were at each other.

She leveled her gaze at him. "What I'm afraid of is you getting into more trouble than I can get you out of, and that's got nothing to do with my personal life."

The barest smile twitched his lips, and he arched one dark eyebrow, both teasing and daring her at the same time. It was that look again, and try as she might, she couldn't make herself back down from it.

"When I was sixteen I met a guy in Barbados—he was older than me, twenty-one, twenty-two—and he followed me home. He sailed into Kingstown one day, wearing that shirt"—she gestured at the T-shirt—"and my dad all but ripped it off his back. Believe me, he didn't stick around long enough to get anything except his hind end kicked."

"What about while you were on Barbados?"

After a moment's thought and assessment, she decided there wasn't any harm in answering. "In Barbados, I lived on my grandparents' sugarcane plantation, which was as close to a convent as you could get without taking the veil. Satisfied?"

Of course he wasn't.

"Is that how you got your name? Because your grandparents own a sugarcane plantation?"

"Not hardly." She gave a short laugh. "They were appalled, still are, but my mom loved it. Sometimes I think the only reason she married my dad, Dr. Thomas Caine, was so she could have a little girl and name her Sugar. Lord knows, the marriage didn't last much longer than it took for me to be born."

"Your parents are divorced?"

"Is this Twenty Questions?"

He gave her a guileless smile that she didn't buy into for a minute. "I'm interested in you." His smile broadened like a wolf's. "Real interested. Is that a crime?"

Warning signals went off up and down her spine, and she answered his first question quickly and succinctly. "Yes, my parents are divorced." She gave herself a mental pat on the back for safely negotiating the waters of her past, then he went and ruined it all.

"What happened to the guy from Barbados?"

Damn him.

It didn't matter, not anymore, she told herself, not

that part of it. And the rest of it would haunt her every day for the remainder of her life whether she answered his question or not.

"He went up-country and fell in love with my mother instead." She gave a slight shrug to mask the pain in her heart, though it wasn't pain from losing a boyfriend. That pain had long since passed. "Don't get anything wrong. My dad never knew, and my mom never knew that I found out or that he'd liked me first. She never would have hurt me like that, never."

"But it hurt anyway."

Her answer was a lift of her own eyebrow. She fought for acceptance of the consequences of her actions, the truly awful ones, the ones she'd done three years after the debacle with the guy from Barbados, every day of her life. She wouldn't let Jackson steal what little peace she'd won. "When you were sixteen, did you lose the girlfriend of your dreams to your much more handsome and sophisticated father?"

He replied with a grin and a shrug of his own, mimicking her. "I never knew my father. I was probably the last thing he and my mother did together." His grin broadened and a mischievous light glinted in his eyes. "As far as losing girlfriends, I don't think it ever happened. I do remember taking a few."

Sugar thought about that for a minute, then slowly nodded. "Yeah, I guess you would."

She was out of her league, way out. Jackson Daniels was the kind of man women shot when he rejected them. She was the kind of woman men forgot.

Strangely, the comparison gave her comfort. She didn't need to worry about anything happening between her and Shulan's half brother. That first night, when he'd said all those crazy things, about how she was the embodiment of all of his fantasies, he'd just been coming down off a heavy dose of narcotics. Lord knows what he'd thought he saw when he looked at her. More than was there, that was for sure.

"Come on," she said, grabbing an orange out of one of the hanging baskets. "From now on, if you don't work, you don't eat. We've got weeds to pull and flowers to pollinate."

"I'm pretty good at pollinating."

She didn't look back to see his smile, but she knew it was there, all over his face, cocky and wry at the same time.

"I just bet you are." She started peeling the orange, dropping the peel in her basket.

He followed her into the cabana, sipping the hot coffee. "You make the best coffee I've ever tasted."

"It's Jamaican Blue Mountain." Finally, she thought with a silent sigh, they'd reached a level of normalcy. Being nice to him was going to pay off. He was already more relaxed, and a relaxed prisoner was less likely to bolt than one pacing on the edge. All she'd had to do was confess a few shaming episodes from her youth, open up a few wounds. The debt she owed Shulan was going to be well and truly paid by the time Jackson Daniels left Cocorico.

"I've heard of Jamaican Blue, but I've never had it

before," Jackson said, watching her deft, slender fingers remove the last of the peel.

"Henry brings it for me, along with a few treats like this." She held up a section of the orange and smiled, a sweet curve of white teeth and impish pleasure, then popped the fruit in her mouth, closing her eyes to enjoy it.

He wasn't sure, but Jackson thought he might just have fallen in love, with her mouth if nothing else, though the possibilities were high on there being something else. She mystified him and fascinated him. Before he'd met her, he wouldn't have put the words *innocent* and *sensual* together, but she embodied them both. In fact, her sensuality was probably the only innocent thing about her. She was guilty as sin when it came to the part she played in his captivity, and as a rule, the pure and the saintly didn't run afoul of people like Fang Baolian.

Still smiling, she opened her eyes. "These are really the best he's ever brought. I've got lime trees, but no oranges." She tore off a piece of the orange and raised it toward her mouth, then seemed to notice him again. "Oh, I'm sorry. Would you like some?" She held the small crescent of fruit out to him.

He could have easily refused the orange, but the woman was irresistible. Without another thought beyond the one that he wanted to touch her with his mouth, steal a kiss however he could, he bent his head and took the fruit from her hand, his teeth grazing the tips of her fingers.

It could be love, he thought, watching the myriad emotions crossing her face, the sudden darkening of her eyes, hearing the small gasp she made when her lips parted in surprise.

It could be love, and that could be the death of him.

FIVE

Sugar was frozen in place, hypnotized by the warmth of his breath and the dampness of his mouth on her fingers. His caress, for it was nothing less and maybe something more, had lasted for mere seconds, but she had to hold herself back from touching him in return, knowing that would be the ultimate confession.

He lifted his head, and the fall of his hair settled back on his chest. A faintly wicked smile curved his mouth as he chewed.

"Tastes good," he said when he was finished. The lazy drift of his gaze partway down her body made her wonder if he meant the orange or her.

When his eyes came back up and locked on hers, the doubt was removed. He meant her. She'd been mistaken when she'd thought the drugs had altered his perceptions. He was stone-cold sober now, and he was looking at her as if she came with whipped cream.

"Yes, well, Henry brought plenty, so help yourself

whenever you'd like one." She took a step backward, clutching her basket to her breasts. "An orange, I mean. Of course."

"Of course." His grin broadened.

She turned around and grabbed a shovel off her tool rack. "You'll need this," she said, thrusting it in his direction. "And this." She gave him a hoe.

"Isn't there something in the Geneva Convention about making prisoners do manual labor?"

"This island doesn't belong to the Geneva Convention." She added a rake to his load. Good Lord, the man had only kissed her fingertips, and she was trembling inside as if he'd started making love to her. "You'll stay in the vegetable garden today. I'll do all the pollina —all the work with the exotics."

He laughed softly behind her. "What happened to the bees? Isn't pollination their job?"

"I'm a little short on bees right now, and some of the plants need insects I don't have. To be on the safe side, I pollinate everything I can." She picked up her pruning shears, putting them in the basket with her gloves, and discreetly sucked in what she hoped was a calming breath before glancing over her shoulder at him. "We'll start in the higher gardens and work our way down."

"What happened to the bees?" he asked, shortening his stride to match hers as they left the cabana and headed up the path.

"A natural disaster." Out in the open air, with plenty of room between them, she regained a measure of her composure. "I went out to the hive one afternoon and found them all dead, or mostly all of them. I think they got into some bad nectar from one of the endangered species, something toxic to their systems."

"Toxic nectar? Sounds like a science-fiction plot," Jackson said. He watched the sun gild her, from the tangled mass of blond curls on top of her head to the curve of her hips and down the length of her legs. With her silvery-gray eyes, peach-colored skin, and blond hair, she was like a beacon of shimmering light drawing him forever onward.

"Oh, it's science, all right. Chemistry. You're looking at chemical warfare on a very grand scale." She swept her hand through the air in front of her, the gesture encompassing all the lush botanical wonders of her home, a place where the plant kingdom had declared a decisive victory.

Houseplants running amok encroached on the courtyard and cradled the trees. Lianas wound through branches and down trunks, snaked their way through shrubs and along the ground, tying all the shades and shapes of green into one photosynthesizing web of life.

"Every plant manufactures compounds to ensure its survival by any and all means available," she continued. "Chemicals to attract, repel, sometimes to kill, sometimes to heal. Many of the species I cultivate are rich in alkaloids or essential oils, the source of a lot of medicines."

She was so lovely, so softly beautiful, that just looking at her nearly broke his heart. "When I was a kid in Hong Kong, our doctor used a lot of herbal treatments, sometimes burning them over us, sometimes pouring them down our throats."

"Hong Kong?" she asked, slanting him a questioning look. "Shulan told me you were American."

The soft slap of their sandals added an even rhythm to the intermittent songs of the flycatchers flitting through the trees. All the sounds of her home were gentle, natural ones. There were no engines, other than the one that ran the generator, and since he'd been there, she'd only used it once, the night she'd turned on the floodlights. There were no cars, no electric hums, no music beyond the lilting tone of her voice.

"Cooper took me back to Asia to live with our aunt when I was still pretty young. Living with his father in San Francisco was hell after our mother died. The old man seemed to hate me more every day of my life."

"Because you were another man's son?" Sugar knew she was trespassing as badly as he had earlier, but like him, she was interested, very interested.

"That was a big part of it, but what really infuriated him was that he couldn't hide the fact that I was some Chinaman's bastard."

"Sun Yi's?"

To her surprise, he laughed. "Shulan sure wants to believe it."

"But you don't?" She kept her eyes on the path and saw a blue-and-green lizard, a jungle runner, skitter across it.

"Even if I did, it wouldn't change what I am or who I am." He lifted his hand and held aside a large fern leaf for her. "Cooper raised me. If I'm anyone's son, I'm his."

"Is he a lot older than you?"

"Ten years. Not much when you think about a six-teen-year-old kid hauling a six-year-old child halfway around the world on his own, without the luxury of two one-way plane tickets."

"You went by ship?" She cast him a disbelieving glance.

"Freighters," he said, reaching into his pocket and pulling out a strip of red cloth that she recognized as the ribbed cuff of an old sweatshirt of hers. More dis-tracting than the red cloth, though, was what putting his hand in his pocket had done to the waistline of the pants. Namely, it had lowered them a good two inches below his tan line, exposing skin a bare shade paler than his chest. She could see the top of one hipbone, which was what she would have sworn was the only thing holding up the pants in the first place. Worse, she could see where the dark hair arrowing down from his navel began to spread across his lower abdomen. Heat infused her senses; he looked so undone.

"Cooper worked for our room and board," he con-tinued, reaching up behind his neck and gathering his hair in one hand. He slipped the red cuff over the single thick cable he'd made and pulled the entire length of his hair through. He repeated the action twice more, until he'd secured everything in a ponytail—and all the while she watched the fluid, rolling action of his muscles and traced the tracks of his veins up the inside of his arm.

Another patch of silky dark hair awaited her there, nestled into a curve of tawny skin.

He was as alluring as any creature she'd ever seen, colorful like a toco toucan with the touch of red in his ebony hair and the amber-streaked green of his eyes, lithe and powerful like the large cats who stalked prey deep in Amazonian forests.

Their next steps took them into a bower of purpleheart and jade vine, two of the indigenous species on Cocorico. The sound of the surf receded into a lulling backdrop, replaced by the calls of birds and the hum of insects. He wasn't for her, she told herself, and she dared not forget it.

"You must have been a six-year-old angel," she said, "to have survived crossing the Pacific on a freighter."

"I was pure hell let loose." He laughed again. "But Cooper was one tough son of a bitch even at sixteen." He paused, as if considering his words, and his expression grew thoughtful before he continued. "He knifed a man on one of the cargo ships, because the guy had me backed into a corner in the engine room, getting ready to . . . well, hurt me. Cooper cut him clean across the back, shoulder to shoulder, and told the guy if he ever caught him in the same room with me again, he would cut out his heart." He held another leaf back for her, the gesture bringing them closer than was good for her control. "Made a helluva impression on me."

"You must have been terrified," she said, forcing herself not to reach out and touch him in compassion, for fear her touch would turn into something altogether different.

"I don't remember being afraid so much as I was confused, not only about what the man said he wanted, but how he could be smiling and crooning at me and smell so evil at the same time."

The image he conjured up struck a responsive chord in her psyche. She remembered what evil smelled like—Fang Baolian. She shuddered.

"It was okay, Sugar, really." He touched her on the shoulder, surprising her with his awareness of the subtle change in her emotions. "He didn't hurt me."

"Did he bother you again?" she asked, allowing him to mistake her momentary weakness for the compassion she hadn't given.

"No. He jumped ship at the next port." The satisfied smile accompanying his answer made her immediately suspicious.

"Why?" she asked.

"Well, it wasn't just because Cooper had sworn to cut his heart out," he admitted, his smile broadening. "I figured if Cooper thought the guy was such bad joss, I ought to take a few stabs at him myself, and being only six, I always got him below the waist. Almost castrated him once."

Her reaction was spontaneous laughter, a big burst of it. What he'd said was terrible and awful—not that he'd hurt the man, but that at six he'd felt the need to protect himself with a knife—but it was also funny.

"I was a real hit-and-run artist," he continued. "I would wait in the gangways, pretending I was the Shadow. Whenever he got within range, I would stick him with my penknife and run like hell, screaming like a banshee for Cooper."

Her laughter faded, but not her respect. "I'm surprised he didn't kill you both in your sleep."

He looked down at her, his smile still in place, but with a cynical edge to it. "He tried, more than once, but Cooper was always quicker and deadlier. He never put a mark on either one of us, but he'd been stitched in half a dozen places by the time we reached the next port."

"You and Cooper must be very close." She knew it was an understatement even as she voiced the thought.

"Maybe too close," he said, his smile gone, replaced by a grimness she found disturbing. "I know Coop, and I know how far he'll go to avenge my death."

"How far?" she asked.

He stopped on the trail and turned her to face him, using a hand on each of her shoulders. His grip was firm but gentle, like his voice when he spoke. "He'll go until he's either broken or dead, and I can't live with that, Sugar. If you can't find it in your heart to let me go, you have to contact him and let him know I'm alive. I tried once from Hong Kong, but got interrupted before I could say much more than his name. A woman had answered the phone, a voice I didn't recognize, so I'm not sure he even knows about the call. But I can't let him get killed because of me, especially when it'd all be for nothing. I'm alive, Sugar, and I want my brother alive."

His hold on her had tightened as he'd spoken, and he'd stepped closer, putting them face-to-face with her head tilted back. The pain in his voice was undisguised, his need clear.

"Do this for me," he said, "and I won't hold you responsible for whatever else happens."

The added incentive was unnecessary. Telling Cooper Daniels his brother was alive wouldn't undermine her promise to Shulan. The cost to her would be in breaking radio silence and upsetting her father, but she had to do it.

"Don't follow me, and he'll know by nightfall," she promised, turning to head back down the path.

Jackson let her go, feeling a weight lift off his shoulders. It would drive Cooper crazy, knowing he was alive, but not knowing where, or how, or when, or if he would be released. But Jackson had spent a lifetime driving Cooper crazy. That part didn't bother him at all, not as long as Cooper was alive.

Sugar went first to her bedroom and pulled a locked box off the top shelf of her closet. Inside the box were Jackson's personal effects: his wallet, a laundry receipt dated four months back, some loose change, a carabiner, a gun, and a used ski-lift ticket. The gun was loaded.

She reached for the wallet and felt a twinge of guilt for prying, but she was doing it for him. The information she needed was simple, a phone number or a fax line, even an address would suffice. She hadn't asked him for it, because she didn't want to give him any idea of how she was going to contact his brother. She didn't want him tearing up the island looking for the source of her communications, a fourth-hand ship-to-shore radio she'd hidden beneath the pantry floor the day he arrived. Not even Jen knew of its existence.

She opened his wallet, prepared to be businesslike, efficient, and objective. She lost all three attitudes when the first thing to fall out was a condom. The foil packet was ancient, the wear and creases almost masking the words printed across the front—*Break Seal in Case of Fire.*

She grinned in spite of herself.

The rest of the contents were less amusing. There was a recent picture of him with a woman. The corners of the photograph were still clean and sharp, the image still clear—and what an image it was. The woman was tall, blond, and willowy, dressed in a sequin-spangled minidress. Jackson was in a tuxedo. The woman's hair was as long as his, drifting to her waist like a waterfall of gold. They made the most striking couple she had ever seen.

She put the photograph aside, wondering if the gorgeous blonde missed him in the night, agonized over where her lover had gone, if he would return. Yet he'd only asked her to contact his brother, no one else.

Also in the wallet was a lot of money and a number of credit cards and business cards, many with notes jotted on them, most having to do with shipping. Judging from the titles of the men and women on the cards, Jackson Daniels was no run-of-the-mill bounty hunter. He dealt with the presidents and CEOs of major shipping corporations and federations. Some of the added notes on the cards were telephone numbers marked with the words *private line.*

The card she was looking for was in a separate compartment of the wallet and read, *Daniels Limited, Maritime Investigations, Jackson Daniels.* Behind that one was another—*Daniels Limited, Investments, Jackson Daniels.* Both listed the same address and phone number in San Francisco, California. Behind the investment card were two cards written in Chinese script. There were two in Arabic, two in Spanish, French, German, and others in languages she could only guess at. Jackson Daniels was definitely more than a bounty hunter; he was an international businessman. The knowledge made her uneasy. Maybe he'd been right that first night on the beach. Maybe she would end up in front of some multinational tribunal for holding him captive. The only thing worse that could happen to her would be for Baolian to find her.

Wallet in hand, she relocked the box and set it back on the shelf. Having a gun on the island did nothing to lessen her uneasiness. Weapons of any kind implied a necessity to use them, and she'd worked hard to ensure the absolute safety of Cocorico. Things were changing faster than she liked.

She also didn't like having to ask her father to call Cooper Daniels and tell him his brother was alive. Thomas Caine's heart deserved better than to be dragged deeper into the mess she'd made of all their lives, and her mother certainly didn't deserve any more grief. Calling her was out of the question. If she got lucky, Carolina would be the one she raised on the radio, but her luck hadn't been running all that good lately.

SIX

Sugar and Jackson were falling into a routine after working together for three days.

"When you've finished turning the compost, you might take some and mulch it around the tomatoes," she said. That was their routine: She gave the orders, he followed them. Usually.

Jackson made a noncommittal sound and continued staring down at the steaming pile of decaying vegetation she'd assigned to him.

"Leaning on the spade isn't going to get the job done."

"Right," he agreed, but didn't make a move.

"Is there something wrong?" she asked, stepping over the rows of cassava she'd been weeding.

"There's something alive in there." They'd been working for hours, mostly on their hands and knees, a position Jackson had been unfamiliar with until she'd put him to work. He played, or had played at, dozens of sports, most of them strenuous, but none of them had prepared him for the drudgery of trying to eke food out of the soil, and none of them had required him to be on all fours. He'd been transformed from a hunter into a gardener, tamed. He was sweating and aching, and he didn't know how she kept at it.

"Sure there is," she said. "About a billion bacteria and a few hundred thousand bugs." She looked at the compost heap, then slanted him a wry glance. "Don't worry. I think you're safe."

"It's bigger than a bacterium, Miss Know-It-All." The irony in his voice matched hers. "I think it's a snake."

She moved a step closer, peering around him. "I doubt it. An island is pretty much a closed ecosystem. I know just about every plant and animal on Cocorico, and believe me, I wouldn't have missed a snake."

"Cocorico?"

"This spot of land you're on in the Windwards, and no, you won't find it listed on any map under that name. Besides, it's too hot in a tropical compost pile for a snake."

"It's not too hot for this one." He poked at the pile, and something indeed moved, quickly, humping up the decomposed vegetable peelings and garden litter.

She swore, a startled sound, and stumbled trying to get away. Jackson automatically slid an arm around her waist, catching her, and her hands grabbed onto him, grappling a hold on his shoulder. Her eyes were wide and locked on the compost heap, her breath short. Their hearts pounded close together for a few glorious, eternal seconds before her common sense reasserted itself, much to his regret. For a second he'd thought his luck had changed.

"Sorry," she said, still somewhat breathless, and disentangled herself from his body. "Don't know what got into me."

He complied with her need for space by relaxing his grip, but he didn't completely let her go. He kept her under the protection of his arm, and when he poked the pile again, she relaminated herself to his side, her arms slipping around his waist and her legs, those sweet legs, coming up against his. Suddenly he had a whole new insight into the Adam and Eve story. He'd bet anything that Adam had asked God to put a snake in the garden, hoping to get Eve sidled up against him. It wasn't anyone's fault that Eve had proven to have more chutzpah than she'd been given credit for having.

He gave the pile another poke.

"Stop doing that!" she cried. "You're going to get it all stirred—" She ended on another softly sworn expletive as the animal responded with a sideways motion of considerable magnitude, sending a wave rippling through the debris like a six-point earthquake. The compost shifted twice more, rippled again for an interminable minute, then was still.

They were quiet for a long time, staring at the compost as if they were waiting for it to do something, either twitch or explode.

Jackson was damn impressed, and curious as hell. If the choice hadn't been between tracking the animal down or holding on to Sugar, he'd already be in the brush.

"Did you ever read *Dune*?" she asked, her knuckles white around handfuls of his shirt.

"Yeah. Twice. The giant sandworms of Arrakis."

"Kind of looked like that, didn't it."

"Yeah."

"Did you actually see it?"

"No, but it moved like a snake, a big one." He felt a shiver course down her spine and turned to see her face. "You're not afraid of snakes, are you?"

"No," she said, releasing him with a shaky laugh. "Sorry about that, grabbing onto you, I mean. It just startled me, that's all." She eyed the undergrowth warily. "I've never seen a snake here before."

"No indigenous species?" He let her go and missed her the moment she stepped away. He'd liked holding her, feeling the aliveness of her in his arms. He'd liked making such a basic human connection.

"No. None," she said, and tucked a stray, damp curl behind her ear.

He'd never seen anyone quite like her. She was both woman and cherub, with her little blunt nose and big gray eyes, with that mass of pale blond curls framing her face like a halo, and a mouth made for love, for kissing and being kissed, soft and slow, hot and deep. She wasn't curvaceous, but the curves she had, at her breasts and hips, beckoned to him.

It seemed as if he'd been alone for years instead of months, away from family, friends, and old lovers who were still good company. He had a few of those in his life. Suddenly he missed them all, everybody, but not quite as much as he missed holding Sugar. The fact was intriguing and disconcerting. The thought of holding her again was arousing.

Even streaked with dirt, she had an elemental and erotic appeal. Her T-shirt and shorts were soft cotton, her skin warm and softer still. He wondered again if Shulan had given him some sort of truth serum designed to make him spill his fantasies, then trapped him here with the only woman who could conceivably make him want to stay.

He wouldn't stay. He would continue to do everything in his power to escape—but the idea had some merit. Who wouldn't want to live in a tropical Eden awash with sunlight and sea foam, and spend his nights making love with a strange and wondrous woman named Sugar Caine?

For if he stayed, that's what it would come down to, sooner or later, and probably sooner. The attraction he felt for her was strong, irresistibly promising. They would become lovers, and he didn't know if that would be a disaster or a blessing.

"There are snakes all over the West Indies, just none here," she said, explaining further, obviously oblivious to the track his mind had taken. "I don't like to think where one might have come from."

He looked out past the vegetable garden, to where her wild plants grew on the other side of the clear, warm stream formed by the waterfall, and the reason for the concern in her voice became clear. Every chance he had depended on winning her over to his side, and he'd just been handed an opportunity.

"Where do you get your plants, the endangered species?"

"Mostly the Amazon."

He nodded and absently poked at the compost. He wasn't going to be making love with her. He was going to leave her and her island as fast as he could figure a way off. "Well, you've pretty much got your pick, then."

"A young boa," she offered.

"Or the tail end of an anaconda."

"Fer-de-lance."

"If you're lucky. A bushmaster if you're not."

"Maybe it just looked big."

He laughed. "Right, and maybe Jen and I better go on a snake hunt."

She caught his gaze. "I wouldn't trust you and Jen to go on an Easter-egg hunt together, and there's no hunting allowed here, not even for renegade snakes."

He laughed again, reaching out and cupping her chin, taking care to be gentle. Touching her skin was like touching satin. Her breath caught, redirecting his attention to her mouth. He watched, fascinated, as her lips parted.

"The only one on this island you can't trust me with is you," he said, attempting to give the words a humorous edge, but failing. His voice had grown too husky to be teasing.

He traced the delicate line of her jaw with his thumb, and her eyes darkened. He was tempted, so damn tempted to take a taste of her mouth. The only thing that stopped him was knowing one taste wouldn't be enough, and that more than one taste would be suicide. The pleasure she offered was of the addicting kind —hot, sweat-slickened skin sliding against his, her scent infusing his senses, and the chance to explore a woman unlike any he'd ever met.

She was ripe with longing. He felt it every time she looked at him. It was part of the mystery of her: why she was alone, how long she'd been alone, how it would feel to ease her loneliness away. It didn't take much imagination to see himself getting lost in loving her, and then losing his opportunity to escape. It was a chance he couldn't take.

The sky darkened around them, warning of the rains to come. Still he hesitated before forcing himself to release her, letting his hand fall back to his side. The first drops hit, splashing warm on his head and shoulders.

"This seems to be happening earlier and lasting longer every day," he said, watching the light of anticipation fade from her silvery eyes. She'd wanted to be kissed, and he hadn't done it. He didn't know which one of them was the bigger fool.

"We're coming up on the full moon." Her lashes lowered and she turned her head away. "The rains on Cocorico follow a lunar cycle. On the night of the new moon, there's no rain at all."

"More science fiction?" he asked, thinking the place was wondrously strange.

"More science fact." Rain splattered her shirt, molding it to her breasts and making his mouth go dry.

"We might as well give it up for the day." She finger-combed her hair, slicking it back off her face. The curls were already damp and growing wetter with every passing second.

He was about to agree, when the skies opened up and dropped a flood. He instinctively reached for her and broke for the trees, her hand gripped in his. They both slipped on the suddenly rain-wet grass and had to fight to gain the protective cover of the forest. Without a word, they headed for the same spot, under the leaves of a giant philodendron growing in the shadow of a châtaignier tree.

It wasn't until they were in the shelter that Jackson realized she was swearing. She had a pretty small repertoire, but then he'd spent a lot of time on docks with men who made regulation sailors look like Sunday-school children.

"If you ever get tired of saying *dammit*, I could teach you a couple of new words," he offered, wiping the water from his face.

"No, thank you . . . dammit."

"I could teach them to you in French." In his experience, women liked French. They responded to it.

"No."

"I can't believe you're sulking over rain. It rains every day." He finished wiping his face and began squeezing the water out of his shirt.

"This is more than rain," she said cryptically.

"Monsoon?"

She shook her head.

"The forty-day-and-forty-night thing with Noah?"

"No."

"Then what's the problem?" he asked.

"When it rains like this within a week of the full moon, the mist gets really heavy around the island, especially at night and early in the morning."

He didn't bother to mention his science-fiction theory again. "There was mist the morning I came. It didn't seem so bad."

"I'm talking about heavy mist, fog. Mist so heavy—" She stopped when the deluge ended as suddenly as it had begun. Raindrops still fell from the sky, but they were separate from each other, distinct, not part of a downpour. She looked out from underneath the green shelter, then crawled forward and rose to her feet. When she was free of the large leaves, she looked back at him. "Maybe I was wrong this time. Don't worry about it."

He hadn't planned on worrying about the mist. He could have told her fog was at the bottom of his current list of problems, but she didn't wait around long enough for him to say anything.

They finished their dinner as the sun was setting to leeward, cassava with a tomatillo sauce, zucchini-and-cheese pie, peach palm, and watermelon. Afterward Sugar made a fresh pot of coffee and carried it out with two cups to the porch table.

"Would you like to try your coffee with coconut milk?" she asked, carefully modulating her voice into a monotone of perfect calmness. He'd almost kissed her, but he hadn't, and she'd been crushed. Foolish heart.

"Please," he said.

The deluge had been the last straw. When she'd first come to the island, the depth and weight of the rare fogs had frightened her. They had been so unexpected, so overwhelming. Gradually, she'd come to accept them, even look forward to them. Their unpredictability made them seem like divinely inspired gifts, a small meteorological remembrance from God to let her know she had not been forgotten.

Jackson would not see it in the same light. He already felt trapped. She didn't want to imagine how much worse it might be for him when the heavy mist settled like a suffocating blanket of white over his world. She had hoped to spare him the experience. He had enough reasons to hate Cocorico and her.

Most of the world didn't know she existed anymore. Jackson Daniels, though, would never forget the woman who'd held him captive in the name of his half sister. She had hoped that sometime, somewhere, he would be able to remember her with more than resentment, or anger, or fear. She had wanted to think he would carry one good memory of his time with her back into the world, but the chances of that were growing slimmer all the time.

Kisses and remembrance. He made her want too damn much.

He thanked her as she set his coffee down, looking up from where he was braiding his hair. The thick strands he worked with were still damp from the shower he'd taken after their work in the garden. The moisture gave his hair an iridescent sheen, making it seem almost blue in its blackness. "Where's Jen?"

"He's been taking his meals at his campsite." Which was where, if she was smart, she would be taking all of her meals. The man couldn't even do the simplest grooming chore without fascinating her.

"Is that what he calls it?"

She let out a short laugh, as much at herself as his question. "I don't know what he calls anything. He hasn't spoken one word to me, not one, but he bows a lot."

"Yeah. I think he bowed to me just before the first time he coldcocked me." A grin teased his mouth as he caught her gaze.

Much to her disgust, she blushed. She should tell him not to smile. It was unnecessary overkill. She was already charmed senseless.

She hated to think she'd throw herself at any man who happened to land on her shores. True, she hadn't been attracted to any of the scientists who had come, but they'd been there for such short times, a morning or afternoon, a full day at the most. They usually came in groups of two or three, half of them were women, and they worked nonstop to gather as much information out of her gardens as they could in their allotted time.

They had not spent hours silhouetting themselves against the seas and skies, looking ever outward as if pure longing could set them free. Jackson Daniels tore at her emotions and her guilt. She felt a responsibility for him, and that responsibility made him seem like hers. Every time he touched her, she felt like she'd been born to be his, a bit of fanciful romanticism that branded her as more foolish than she would have thought possible a week ago.

"Is that why you call this place Cocorico?" he asked, running his finger through the stream of creamy milk she was pouring into her cup. "Because of the coconuts?"

"No." She watched him suck the liquid off his finger and cleared her throat before going on about her business. "A cocorico is a bird, a rufous-vented chachalaca."

He picked up his coffee and took a sip, holding the nearly finished braid in his other hand. "This is good, really good."

"I'm glad you like it. Sometimes I put chocolate in, too, but I'm out of chocolate right now."

"When will you get more?" He brought the cup back to his mouth.

"In a few weeks." She'd been about to say, Not until after you leave, but she'd caught herself in time. She didn't want to remind him of one more thing he didn't have control over in his life.

"Are you telling me that I'm trapped here without chocolate?"

The dismay in his voice brought a reluctant smile to her lips. "If I can survive it, you can."

"I don't know, Sugar. You don't know me and chocolate. We're real close."

He was trying so hard to be casual and friendly, she thought, it was making her feel like a charity case. Kissing each other would have been a terrible mistake, but he could at least have the decency not to be cheerful.

"You can't love it any more than I do," she said, "and I always make it between shipments. Though I usually don't run out this quickly."

"What happened this time? Did you go on a chocolate-eating marathon?" Using a piece of string she'd given him, he tied off the end of his braid and tossed it over his shoulder.

She'd never known a man to have such wonderful hair. It made her own short locks seem particularly inadequate. With a self-conscious gesture, she ran her fingers through one side of her hair, trying to fluff up the curls.

"No," she said, stifling a sigh. It was hopeless. A person couldn't possibly fluff up a few inches of blond hair to look like a silken veil. "Henry happened this time. He usually only comes twice a month, but I think he's fallen in love with Carolina, so all the time she was here, he kept showing up. And every time he showed up, I was out a little more chocolate."

"Who is Carolina?" he asked, and Sugar could have kicked herself.

"A friend," she said in a tone to discourage further questions.

He either missed her warning inflection or chose to ignore it.

"Henry says she's beautiful and cruel."

The description was so outlandish it made her laugh, that and the relief she felt that he'd already known about Carolina. She'd still made a mistake, but she hadn't given him any new information.

"Cruel? Carolina? Lord, Henry must have it bad." She leaned back in her chair and took a sip of her coffee.

"What are his chances with her?" Jackson asked.

She shook her head. "Not good. Carolina already had one rummy for a husband. Fortunately, as so often happens, he ran off with another woman who thought he was worth all the trouble he caused. Carolina prays for her every night out of gratitude, and she isn't likely to take to another drunk."

When he didn't immediately ask another question, she allowed herself to relax her guard and tried not to settle back into moroseness.

She understood his need for answers. He was trying to piece his new world together, but she was afraid of those damn slipups of hers, of giving him more information than was safe. His freedom was less than a hundred yards from the cottage, on the other side of the cliffs. If he ever discovered the pirate's door, he could literally walk away, get on her boat, and disappear.

And he would do just that. She didn't have a doubt. Cocorico wasn't big enough to hold him. Lord, some days, and lately some nights, it barely held her.

A hummingbird zipped up to the bougainvillea shrub growing at the side of the cottage, hovered for a few seconds above the flowers, and zipped away. Another one soon took its place. The nightly chorus of tree frogs began up by the cliffs, adding a syncopated backbeat to the pounding of the surf. And so went the cycle of her island life. The only difference tonight was the man sharing her table.

She sneaked a glance at him and found him staring at her with an intensity that caused her to flush. She quickly looked away, but the image of his eyes, green with the reflected fire of the sunset, remained in her consciousness and kept her heart from slowing down to normal.

"Is that what happened to you?" he asked, all traces of friendliness burned away by the edge in his voice. "Did your husband run off with Baolian, and she wanted the ex-wife out of the way?"

"No." Her hands tightened on her coffee cup. She should have been able to laugh at the outrageous question, but his harsh tone made laughter impossible.

"Did one of Baolian's lovers leave her for you?" There was a hesitation in his words, as if he found the question particularly distasteful.

She didn't answer him. The day was going to end with tension and angry words. She wasn't going to wait around for the complete deterioration. She was leaving, but before she could make more than a tentative move, he captured her arm with his hand.

"Did one of Baolian's lovers leave her for you?" he repeated.

He wasn't hurting her, but the strength of his grip told her she wasn't going anywhere.

"No," she said, forcing herself not to flinch. In the days he'd been there, she'd forgotten what he was in the real world—a man who hunted the scum of the earth and either took them down or brought them in for money. A man like that wasn't to be pitied or taken lightly, or sighed over in her sleep.

His hold on her relaxed the barest of degrees.

"Tell me what your connection to Baolian is," he said, "and don't bother to lie. I'll know. The people I usually deal with are the best liars in the world."

Despite the true danger he represented, she shot him a resentful glance. "I am not one of the people you usually deal with. Now let me go."

"When you tell me why you're here."

"It doesn't concern you."

She was wrong, Jackson thought, and he didn't like it any better than she did.

"Everything about you concerns me," he said, leaning forward across the table, his patience coming to an unexpected end. Baolian was a viper, and she had this woman in her grasp. He wanted to know why. He wasn't going to let her go until he found out.

"I'll scream for Jen."

The threat was real and formidable, but Jackson wasn't taking delivery. "Leave Jen out of this. This is between you and me."

Her lashes lowered in a gesture of defeat—or so he thought. He should have known better. Women had their own weapons, and hers cut him to the quick.

"Shulan wouldn't have brought you here if she had thought you would hurt me, and I trusted her judgment." Gray eyes lifted to meet his. "I'm supposed to be safe here, Jackson. Don't take that away from me too."

She spoke quietly and with absolute conviction, putting him to shame, something he would have thought impossible before he'd dropped out of the sky and onto her island. He'd actually hurt people and felt less guilt than he did just for holding her wrist.

He released her and slumped back into his chair, watching her leave and wondering what in the hell else he'd taken from her. He couldn't think of a damn thing, certainly nothing that counted. Not her kiss, not the feel of her in his arms, not the sweetness of his name on her lips.

For hours after she'd left him, he sat alone, his thoughts as dark as the night closing in around him.

SEVEN

He wanted to howl at the moon. He threw rocks instead, skimming jagged chunks of limestone over the tops of the waves. He'd seen her light come on after the sun had dropped into the western sea. He didn't know how she survived this damn place. It was making him stir-crazy. There were no amenities, no communications, no distractions—except for her.

Sugar. He threw another rock as far out into the ocean as he could. The cargo boat was out there again, plying the waters on its rounds, just out of his reach.

The night had been endless after she'd left. He'd sunk so low as to hike up to Jen's icehouse for company. Surprisingly, he'd found some. But the man was old, and the conversation had run out about the same time as the tea.

So now he was alone again, on the beach, throwing rocks and still feeling like a jerk. The hell of it was, he hadn't done anything. Most of the time when he asked a question of a criminal—and that's what she was in this instance—he got an answer, one way or another.

Growing up a half-caste hadn't been easy in Hong Kong, not even with the protection of the money and respectability provided by his mother's family. Without Cooper, or the threat of Cooper, he would have lost more fights than he'd won in the back halls of the private schools he'd attended. Once he'd gotten out of short pants, the odds had started changing in his favor, and before Cooper had left Hong Kong to make his own fortune, he'd made damn sure his little brother could take down anybody he might run up against in school or in a Hong Kong alley.

He never referred to himself as a "lean, mean fighting machine," but Cooper did, usually when he was on top, holding Jackson down in some god-awful body lock.

Cooper would have gotten answers out of Sugar. He wouldn't have backed down just because she'd looked up at him with big gray eyes. The woman was making him soft.

Right. Jackson swore and let out a harsh laugh. She wasn't making him soft. She was making him hard, and that was his biggest problem.

He threw his last rock, knowing he had a choice to make. He could either stand there and slowly go out of his mind, or he could do something.

He decided to do something, beginning with stripping off his shirt. Then he went for his pants, pulling on the drawstring to loosen the material around his hips.

———◆————————◆———

Sugar straightened from where she'd been leaning against the bungalow's doorjamb, watching Jackson and the *Mary Sue*. For a moment she wondered what he was doing. By the time she'd crossed the verandah and his pants had fallen into the sand, she knew.

Her heart skipped a beat. She'd been expecting him to come up with something ever since she and Jen had destroyed his raft. But not this.

"No," she gasped, racing for the beach stairs.

Halfway down, she shouted his name and saw him turn from where he was in the water with the waves breaking against his waist.

Jackson looked up the beach, thinking he'd heard her call his name and wondering just how much wishful thinking it took to make a fantasy a reality. Then he saw her, running across the sand in the moonlight.

The night breeze and the surf kept her words from carrying to him, but he heard distress in her voice and responded, lunging out of the water.

He caught her to him while still knee-deep in the sea. She put her hands on his forearms and pulled, breathlessly swearing at him.

"Dammit, Jackson . . . You can't . . . I told you."

The receding water pushed her up against him and nearly knocked her over. To save them both a dunking, he swung her up into his arms and strode out of the surf. On the short walk from the ocean to where he'd left his pants, it crossed his mind no fewer than a hundred times that he was naked and she was lying up against him.

"Jackson." She held on to him as he set her on her feet. "You . . . you—" Words failed her as she gulped for breath.

"Are you okay?" he asked, cutting right to the chase, his hands gripping her as tightly as she was gripping him.

"Yes." She nodded. "Couldn't sleep . . . saw you in the water . . . sharks."

That's what this was about? he thought. Sharks? The adrenaline rush she'd given him dissipated, leaving him with an awareness of other things, like the feel of her silk shirt beneath his palms. He'd slept in silk a few times. Silk sheets.

"I know about the sharks, Sugar," he assured her. "They don't come into this stretch of water, this close to the shoreline. The rockslides on both ends of the beach act as a reef."

He was right, but Sugar was surprised he'd figured it out.

"At low tide," he continued, "you can even see rocks sticking up about fifteen yards out. Nothing too big is going to want to get trapped in this little bay. If it did, we would have it for supper."

"Then you knew not to go any farther." She'd caught her breath, but her heart was still pounding, and she still had a good grip on his arms, in case he had any more crazy ideas. "You weren't trying to swim out to the boat? To get away?"

When he shook his head, she felt the first inklings of

vexation seep into her mind. She'd practically killed herself in her mad dash down the beach to keep him from throwing his life away in an unkind ocean, and apparently all for nothing.

"I've been swimming every night, but not away," he said.

"You've been swimming every night?" She didn't want to believe it. He'd been swimming every night and she hadn't known. Whatever in the hell was he going to do next? "Don't you—don't you know there are things other than sharks in these waters!" She gave him a shake, or as much of one as she could, considering their size difference. "Anything could have gotten you. Anything! You could have been bitten, stung, poisoned, sliced to ribbons—"

"Sugar." He spoke her name quietly, but she refused to be calmed down.

"Portuguese man-of-war, moray eels, coral, sea urchin. You name it, it's out there. And we haven't even gotten to the fog. It is not polite stuff, Jackson. When it rolls in, it comes like the tsunami from hell. Three yards from the beach, and you'd never make it back. You are my responsibility, and as long as you're here, I forbid you to swim at night."

She knew she was ranting, but damn, he'd scared her. She lowered her gaze to take a calming breath, and suddenly noticed he was naked. In an instant she let him go. The air went out of her lungs on a gasp and her gaze flew up his body. "You're naked."

"Forbid?" he repeated with an arched eyebrow and a who-the-hell-are-you attitude. "There's only one thing you can forbid me, Sugar, and that's only because I'm civilized enough not to want it unless you give it."

She knew what *it* he was talking about, and her cheeks flamed. "Civilized people do not take their clothes off at every opportunity," she informed him with as much authority as she could muster.

It wasn't enough.

"I wouldn't badmouth the civilization of my nature, if I were you," he warned. "Next to Jen, it's the only protection you've got."

"I—I can take care of myself." She took a step back, only to realize it exposed more of him to her view. "You've got to— Oh, here." Exasperated, she reached down and whipped his pants up off the beach. With her head turned aside, she stuck them out in his direction. "Put your clothes on."

"What's the magic word?"

She gritted her teeth, not knowing why she was so worried about the sharks. The way things stood, she'd probably end up killing him herself.

"Please."

She felt him take the pants out of her hands and heard him snap out the sand.

"Okay," he said a minute later. "I'm decent."

"No, you're not." She started walking up the beach, embarrassed by her overreaction and disheartened by their harsh words. He'd been offended by her laying down the law, and she had to concede him that right. She wasn't his boss, but she was responsible for him. It was an impossible situation.

Much to her chagrin, he fell in step beside her.

"I thought you were taking a swim," she said, lengthening her stride.

"I thought you forbade me to swim."

He was mocking her. That made her angry all over again, but this time the anger was more awful; it was the kind where she cried. He seemed to have a remarkable talent for making her feel foolish.

"I hate fighting with you." She tightened her hands into fists and stared straight ahead, trying not to blink, hoping that would hold back the tears.

"Then we have a lot in common," he said. "I hate fighting with you too."

She didn't believe him. He must love fighting with her, because she was always the one who gave in and ran off. She wasn't used to losing, not on Cocorico. She wasn't used to sharing either, and it had been clear from the beginning that her home wasn't big enough for both of them.

"We don't have anything in common," she disagreed. "And that's the problem. I don't know what to do with you." She mounted the first step of the beach stairs, hoping to leave him behind. He stopped her with his hand on her shoulder, though, and turned her around.

"More in common," he said, standing in the sand in front of her, resignation softening his voice. "Because I sure as hell don't know what to do with you either."

Within the space of the next breath, the tension between them changed, deepened, became less mentally agitated and more potently sensual.

"I know what I'd like to do with you," he continued,

his gaze drifting over her face. When he got to her mouth, he grinned wryly, then he raised his eyes to meet hers again. "But that's bound to end up being more trouble than fighting."

Her heart was in her throat—and his hand was gliding up to cup the back of her neck, mesmerizing her. He was going to kiss her.

"I usually know who the bad guys are," he went on, "but with you I can't tell." He tunneled his fingers through the hair at her nape, sending a shiver of anticipation down her spine. "You're not like any pirate I ever busted, but you're the one keeping me here."

"I'm not a bad guy." She could hardly breathe for the way he was looking at her, the verdant hue of his eyes darkening with desire, his mouth softening as his smile faded.

He tightened his hold on her ever so slightly, drawing her forward. "But are you a good girl, Sugar? That's what I really want to know."

She never got the chance to answer. He lowered his mouth to hers, and every dream she'd ever had came to life: of his breath mingling with hers, of his strength surrounding her, of being with him.

So this was what it felt like to kiss him. Heaven.

Her lips parted on a soft moan, and he deepened the kiss, sucking on her tongue. A bolt of shock and pleasure ricocheted through her body, spreading a wildfire of desire. She opened her mouth wider and did the same to him, only slower, more tentatively, and desire doubled over on itself and pooled in her loins.

His hand slid to her waist, urging her closer with

each act of suction and release, until she was flattened against him from breast to thigh, laid up against his body like a lover.

The dampness of his pants soaked through her shorts, making it easier to feel him, and something inside her quickened. He stroked her lips with his tongue, and she gasped from the sheer erotic pleasure of touching him and being touched.

He tasted of salt and man, his mouth so mobile and skilled, she knew he had done this thousands of times—kissed a woman and made her ache from wanting to know more of him. His heart beat strongly beneath her palm, his body hard, his skin like satin, the dragon's fire warming her even as his kiss made her burn. She wanted to kiss him forever.

Jackson groaned. Calling the woman in his arms Sugar wasn't even half-right. She was more than sweet. She was nectar, the lure leading to procreation. Kisses were not going to be enough to satisfy him, not even her hot, wild kisses. He wanted to be inside her.

He lowered his hand from her waist to her buttocks and pressed her into his groin. Her response was to melt against him in all the wonderful ways of a woman, opening herself with softness, cradling him . . . driving him past the edge of reason.

Pure instinct guided him as he thrust against her, gently ground his pelvis against her. She trembled, her mouth stilling under his for a heartbeat. With the feel of her breath warming his lips, he thrust again, deliberately, his body asking a question his mind was past formulating. When she responded with an answering pressure, her tongue delicately exploring his, he released whatever shred of restraint he might have had left.

Sugar felt the change in him, the tightening of his muscles, the extra degree of heat in his touch, and she knew she was playing with fire. Except kissing him wasn't a game, and his responses only made her want more. She wasn't a good girl. She was a woman who had been alone too long, a woman who had never known anyone she'd wanted as much as she wanted him.

If she could have asked for one man to come to Cocorico, she would have asked for someone like him, someone daring, a man with an ingrained instinct to protect, a fighter with the courage to stand unafraid under a master's sword, a man who kissed with both lust and tenderness in a way that broke her heart with more wanting.

He wasn't hers, though. He could never be hers, no matter how much she wanted him, no matter how much she took from him this night. She kissed him again, tasting him and putting the taste in her memory, which was all she would ever really have of him. She ran her hand up his chest, feeling the wonder and strength of him. She traced his jaw with her fingertips and let her fist close around a silky handful of his hair. Through it all, she told herself to remember . . . remember . . . the taste and feel and scent.

Jackson thought he was in paradise. Her hands were all over him, her kisses growing desperate, and then he felt the tears running down her face.

She was crying.

That had never happened to him before. Never, not once. He wanted to keep kissing her, hoping the tears would go away. When she made a soft sobbing sound, he knew his luck had run out, again. The sensual lust he'd been priming, the excitement pumping through his veins, the sweet clean edge of anticipation, all of it drained out of him, leaving him empty and yearning. The familiar thrill hadn't lasted nearly long enough, and they'd barely had a chance to get to the best part, the unfamiliar thrills.

There was no help for it, though, not when she was crying.

Silently cursing himself for being a thousand times a fool, he ended the kiss with a soft brush of his lips across hers and gathered her into his arms. She was supple and lean, strong in her own way, but small. Her hair smelled of rainwater and hibiscus, and her tears were making long, hot tracks down his chest. It all made him want to hold her that much closer.

They made a fine pair, he thought, trapped together in a tropical Eden with no way out and damn little to offer each other.

A few more days of paradise and he'd be praying for Shulan to come back, preferably with the brute, Sher Chang, at her side. Then he'd at least have something and someone to fight and a clear idea of who the bad guys were on the island.

Fighting with Sugar was no good. Kissing her, if it made her cry, was even worse. Jen was pretty much washed up as an opponent. The only way he'd get a fight out of the old man, verbal or otherwise, was if he hurt Sugar, an idea even more contrary to his nature than celibacy.

He ran a hand down her back and wished she didn't feel so good. Another sob broke from her, and he wished she didn't feel so bad.

"If I promise not to kiss you again, will you stop crying?" he asked, wanting to help her and not knowing how. He wasn't experienced with women's tears, mostly because he'd never stuck around to watch any, let alone get wet from them. He and Cooper had always lived in a man's world—no children, no permanent women, and a mother who had died too young to impart the gentler emotions to her sons.

Sugar shook her head, refusing his offer. He didn't know whether to be relieved or resigned.

"If I kiss you again, will you stop crying?" One of his better ideas, he thought, but she again answered with a negative shake of her head.

Great. Now he was not only sexually frustrated and physically miserable, he was confused.

"It's not you," she murmured against his chest, where her tears were threatening to drown his dragon. "It's not your fault."

If she thought she was making him feel better, she'd missed the mark by a mile. He liked to think he was still capable of making an impact on a situation, especially one in which he was intimately involved.

Not knowing what else to do, but knowing he wasn't ready to let her go, he lowered his head and kissed the smooth curve of her brow, whispering words of solace.

"Shhh. Don't cry, Sugar. Everything will be all right." And it would be, everything all right, if she would only give him his freedom—and let him give her his loving.

He felt the sighed release of her breath on his chest and moved to kiss the tears off her cheek, taking surprising pleasure in the task of comforting. Her skin was soft, both salty and sweet on his tongue.

She sighed again. As he buried his face in her hair, filling himself with her fresh, exotic scent, his thoughts of comforting were swamped with renewed desire. She had to know how good it could be between them.

"I'm sorry," she said. "I promise this won't happen again."

Her voice was so quiet, he almost didn't hear her. When her words sank in, he wished he hadn't.

She pushed away to leave, and not having a choice, he let her go. He stayed on the beach while she climbed the stairs to her bedroom to sleep alone.

As for him . . . Ah, hell, he wasn't going to sleep at all.

EIGHT

Sugar awoke to the warm and fragrant smells of coffee and fruit, and something else so distinctive and wonderful, but so unexpected, she couldn't, and didn't, believe her nose. She did allow herself to entertain the impossible and rolled onto her side, sniffing the air, though not daring to open her eyes and shatter the sensory illusion. It had to be an illusion. No one could have delivered freshly baked cinnamon rolls to her bedroom.

Yet the scent stayed strong and sure and yummily spicy, wafting through the air. She stretched lazily on the bed, all the while wondering what exotic plant could have bloomed in her garden to create the enticing smell of cinnamon. There were so many flowers on Cocorico, all of them fragrant.

Maybe tomorrow she would bake something good for breakfast. Today, she was disappearing, sneaking off to the other side of the island to be alone. She'd had enough of men. A white sand beach and clear aquamarine water awaited her in her hideaway, along with the solitude she needed to reclaim, if only for a few hours.

She sniffed the air again, inhaling the spice scent and the aroma of Jamaican Blue Mountain—and suddenly it occurred to her that the smell of coffee in her bedroom should have been as impossible as cinnamon rolls. If one was there, why not the other? And if both, how?

She hazarded a peek at the bedside table, less than a foot away. There was coffee all right, and sliced papaya, and the unbelievable cinnamon rolls. She closed her eyes and stifled a small groan into her pillow. Someone had been in her room while she slept. That someone would not have been Jen. He didn't drink coffee, and he wouldn't have dared to trespass. He lived on green tea and privacy. That someone could only have been Jackson Daniels.

Another groan escaped her. Jackson loved her coffee, all things sweet, and he would have dared anything. She slowly opened her eyes again. From the look of it, he also knew how to bake incredibly decadent cinnamon rolls.

She extended her hand and ran a finger through the caramelized goo of butter and sugar pooled on the plate. The syrup was still warm from the oven. So was the small piece of roll she tore off. He must have just been in her room.

A blush crept up her cheeks, reminding her of why she was hiding out for the rest of the day. She couldn't face him, not after he'd kissed her. Not today, maybe not ever, even considering how difficult, actually impossible, that would be with the two of them trapped on the same small plot of land. She couldn't get away from him until Shulan came and took him away—unless she let him go.

She swore softly at the thought. Jackson Daniels was playing hell on her loyalties and her values. She had to keep reminding herself that Shulan was only trying to protect him. She had to do the same.

The syrup made a slow track off the roll, running onto her finger. She hurriedly stuck the piece of roll in her mouth to keep from getting cinnamon goo on the bed. Her eyes widened briefly at the first bite, then drifted closed in ecstasy.

The tastes in her mouth were ambrosial, exquisite, imploding on her senses and melting away her discouraging thoughts. She sank back into her pillows. The man could cook.

She reached over and tore off another piece of roll, thinking she ought to hide him from Shulan just to keep him there. Any man who baked cinnamon rolls in the morning and delivered them, fresh, hot, and divine to a woman's bedside, was worth keeping.

On the other hand, any woman who kept Jackson Daniels just because he could cook, probably needed her head examined. The man needed nothing more than his kiss, no more talent than what it took to hold a woman in his arms, to make him of rare value.

A secret smile played across her lips. She'd loved his kiss, the way he'd tasted, and being wrapped in his arms with his body hot and hard against hers. It wasn't his

fault all of that hadn't been enough. The truth had surprised even her.

All these years on Cocorico, she'd dreamed of having someone to love. When Jackson had been delivered
to her, young, strong, beautifully masculine, and exotic
enough to entice, she'd thought her dreams had come
true.

When he'd kissed her, though, she had realized it
wasn't enough that he was all she'd dreamed of and that
he wanted her. Suddenly she had wanted love, the forever kind. It hadn't been good enough to know he
would be there in the morning, simply because he
couldn't get away. She needed to know he would be
there when the fruit trees bloomed again, and when it
was time to harvest the cassava, and only because he
would never want to leave her.

Making love with him without having his love would
have been an unmitigated disaster—even though it
would have been incredibly glorious. Her secret smile
returned, a little sadder, but no less dreamy. She didn't
have a doubt it would have been glorious.

Jackson sat motionless in the shadows of her room,
every nerve ending on fire with the pure, unadulterated
wanting of her. He'd never seen anyone awake so sensu-
ously, using touch, taste, brief glances of sight, and
smell to explore her morning world. He wanted to be
the focus of all that attention, especially touch and taste.
He wanted to be the one to suck the sugar off her fingers and then keep going until he'd covered every inch
of her.

She bent her knee into the air while eating another

piece of cinnamon roll, and his gaze followed a heated path up the newly exposed inside of her thigh. A scrap of cotton hid her most private place from his view, and he was grateful. He could hardly breathe as it was for the ache she'd started in him. Any more voyeuristic pleasures and he'd do something rash—like pounce on her.

"Mmmmm," she murmured, licking her fingers, her knee swaying back and forth.

"I'm glad you like it." His voice was so hoarse, he hardly recognized it as his own.

Sugar didn't have any trouble recognizing the voice. She shot up in the bed.

"You," she gasped.

"Me," he admitted.

He was half-hidden in the shadows darkening the far corner of the bedroom, lazily gracing a rattan chair with his hands clasped across his stomach and his legs spread wide, watching her with a predatory gleam in his eyes.

"What are you doing in here?" she demanded, working a fair amount of righteous indignation into her words.

"Thinking."

"About what?" she asked incredulously.

Sex, he wanted to say, the sex we didn't have last night, but he doubted if telling her the truth was in his best interest.

"I thought we could talk," he said instead.

Sugar couldn't believe his audacity. He'd not only come into her room uninvited, he'd hung around and watched her sleep. Exactly what she had done to him when he'd first arrived, she thought with a little twinge of guilt. A very little twinge. "I don't want to talk."

"Good." A sensual smile curved across his face, and in one lithe movement, he was out of the chair and coming for her.

She scrambled back to the head of the bed, clutching at the sheet she'd worked off during the night and jerking it up to her chin.

"Does that really make you feel safer?" he asked, dropping down on the bed and gesturing at the sheet crumpled in her fingers.

"What would make me feel safer is if you left. You shouldn't have come in here in the first place." Her self-righteous indignation had done a nosedive into crossness, and it was all his fault. She could have held on to the high ground if he'd stayed put on the other side of the room. This close, her reaction to him couldn't be ignored, and it irritated her no end.

"I thought you might like breakfast in bed for a change," he said. "And from what I could see, I think I was right."

He was baiting her and raising her internal temperature to a sultry simmer at the same time. Bands of light from the partially opened jalousies streaked his face and body, revealing the teasing light in his eyes and the bareness of his chest. The dragon looked particularly content this morning, stretched across a landscape of beautifully defined muscle, basking in the sunshine . . . warming his heart with flames of red and gold.

He'd kissed her, and she knew he would kiss her

again if she offered the slightest encouragement. It was a heady power, a tantalizing choice, but unlike him, she wasn't one who dared anything and the consequences be damned.

She slowly lifted her gaze to meet his, determined to neutralize the tension, the situation, and her own wayward emotions. "You were right. Thank you."

A polite *thank you* should have cooled his ardor, but Jackson had underestimated the mistake he'd made by getting so close to her, close enough to feel the warmth of her body and smell the woman's scent of her.

They were on her bed, with her hair all tousled from sleep and her eyes still soft from dreaming. The silk shirt he'd felt in the night was midnight blue and nearly half off one shoulder, exposing a delectable expanse of skin darkened to a golden hue by the sun.

He should have swum last night as if his life depended on it, because he was beginning to believe it might, what with the innocent-erotic magic of Sugar Caine working on him, pulling him ever deeper into the place where she nurtured her gardens and tracked the moon across the sky each night. More than any machinations by Shulan, it was Sugar who could keep him on the island, bind him more securely than chains and threats.

He'd never once thought he could make love with her and not be changed. Every woman he'd ever loved had changed him, whether they'd physically consummated their feelings or not. He didn't believe in sex without love, but he'd be the first to admit that love was easy to conjure up when fueled by desire.

Sugar was different, though, what he felt for her was different. He'd never been afraid of a woman, but she scared the hell out of him—and it still wasn't enough to make him run.

"I found a honey jar marked *Before the Bees Died* in the pantry and used some of it." He leaned over and helped himself to a slice of papaya, bringing them very close for the eternal span of a heartbeat.

He offered her the fruit, but her eyes shifted away from him to where she was fingering the sheet in her lap. For an instant, no more, he allowed himself to wonder how much of his soul a second kiss would cost. Then he ate the papaya himself.

"I thought I tasted the wildness of honey," she said, creasing the sheet with a fingernail, seemingly absorbed in the task.

He wanted to tell her he'd tasted a wildness in her kiss, but the price was too high, even for mere words. He couldn't play at love with her and hope to win. In truth, he couldn't win at all. If he stayed and touched her, if he whispered what he feared was in his heart, he was lost. If he left, he was condemned to burn with a desire no other woman could appease.

He would be a fool to strengthen her hold on him any more.

"Yeah, well," he said, "before things get any wilder around here, I think we should discuss a few alternatives." He deliberately put an edge in his voice to fight the tenderness welling up inside him. God, she was the most dangerous thing on two legs he'd ever been up against, including Fang Baolian. The Dragon Whore had only wanted his body. Sugar was consuming him, mind, body, and soul.

"What alternatives?"

He didn't miss the wariness in her voice, but he did nothing to assuage her suspicions. It was time to lay his cards on the table.

"I give you money, and you help me leave. Clean, simple, and effective." He left out the word *painful*. The last thing he wanted was to feel pain at leaving her. She was a stranger, nothing more than a beautiful stranger.

When she didn't respond except to look at him with increased doubt, he sweetened the pot.

"Think about it, Sugar. No more extra mouth to feed, no one you have to save in the middle of the night, no more questions to answer." Despite his best intentions, his voice softened and he let his gaze trail over her from shoulder to thigh. Damn her for being what she was, for making him throw caution to the wind. "No more hot kisses on the beach keeping you up half the night because all you got was kisses." He took a rough breath, forcing his gaze above her waist. "No more waking up with a man in your room who's been watching you sleep and wondering how good it could be if he took off his clothes and lay down beside you."

The color in her face heightened and spread down across her chest.

"All you have to do is name your price. I can meet it."

"I can't be bought," she said, stubbornly refusing to meet his eyes.

"How much is Shulan paying you?"

"Nothing. I'm the one who owes her."

A hundred questions came to mind with her statement, but he didn't ask them. He just waited.

"Whatever you're thinking, you're probably wrong," she said after a few moments of uncomfortable silence, her eyes flicking up to his.

"I'm thinking about sex," he said, as much to tell her the truth as to throw her a curve. "But if you want me to think about something else, feel free to make a suggestion . . . or a confession."

She drew her knees in tighter to her chest, a bit of body language with only one interpretation: She was battening down the hatches.

Jackson silently conceded defeat. His only consolation was in knowing it hadn't been the mention of sex that had put her on the defensive. It had been the mention of a confession. She hated to give away her secrets, and to her everything about herself and Cocorico was a sacred secret.

"I thought I'd look for the snake today," he said, changing the subject. His attempt at bribery had failed, so far, and he knew he wasn't going to get anywhere by intimidating her. "If I get lucky, maybe we could cook it up for dinner."

"Dinner? My snake?" He had definitely gotten her attention.

"Your snake?"

Her face took on a rebellious expression. "I meant what I said, Jackson. No hunting. If it's here on the island, no matter how it got here, I have a responsibility to care for it."

Her words rang with more conviction than he'd ever heard offered in the name of a reptile. He wondered if she felt the same about dragons.

"If it's a bushmaster, it doesn't need all that much care, just a little fresh meat every now and then," he said, still curious, but trying to be reasonable. "The same goes for an anaconda or a boa. I'd just like to make sure the fresh meat isn't one of us, either by accident or design."

"I don't know how anything as big as an anaconda or a boa constrictor could have gotten on the island," she said, dismissing at least half of his theory, the less dangerous half by his estimation.

"And a bushmaster?"

"Nearly as impossible. They're not exactly small."

"Well, I don't know how you could have gotten on the island either, but you're here," he countered, clearly open to an explanation.

One she obviously wasn't going to give. "You can't kill my snake."

He gave up. "No snake killing, no swimming. You're not leaving me much for entertainment, Sugar, unless you had something else in mind." He considered giving her a wicked grin, then thought better of the idea.

"You're not here to be entertained."

She had a point, but he wasn't there to get himself tangled up with another woman either, and that was certainly happening.

"Okay, I won't kill the snake," he agreed, the wicked grin slipping through his better intentions. "But if you feel something slither up to you in the middle of the night and it doesn't answer to my name, you better jump."

He pushed himself off the bed, gratified by the shock widening her eyes. He leaned down and with feigned casualness brushed his mouth across hers. It was a hell of a chance to take, but he had to kiss her; and as he'd feared, one kiss wasn't enough. Time slowed within the space of a pulse beat, his smile faded, and of their own accord his hands came up and molded themselves to her shoulders, his fingers straying across her bared skin.

"Sugar," he whispered, her name a reverent question on his lips. He hated revealing his weakness for her, and he would have left if she'd given any sign of wanting him to leave.

She didn't.

Her lashes fell in feathery crescents to her cheeks, her breath caught, and he was captured—so easily.

So easy to push the silk shirt completely off her shoulder. So easy to let his gaze slide over the bared tops of her breasts. It would be so easy to lower her to the bed and follow her down, to fit his body to hers and let the thrill of contact flood his senses and fill his heart. So damn easy to put himself at her sweet mercy.

He curled his hands into fists and pulled away. Nothing short of a miracle was going to keep him sane and celibate much longer.

Sugar felt his withdrawal and opened her eyes to watch him leave, all macho arrogance and graceful strength dressed in nothing except the loose, flowing black cotton pants. He was so much stronger than she.

The plan she'd had to befriend him had proven to be dangerously absurd. Her only hope of surviving him, of keeping herself from begging him for his touch, was to avoid him at all costs. She couldn't have him for keeps, so she was better off not knowing what she was missing.

Her body called her a liar and a fool. It wanted him at any cost, but her heart was adamant in its denial.

She reached over and picked up a slice of the papaya he'd brought for her. The fruit was sweet and silky in her mouth—the way his tongue had been when he'd kissed her on the beach. The way she'd hoped it would be again only moments before.

She reached for another slice of fruit and savored it slowly, remembering. She could fall in love with his kiss, maybe with more than his kiss.

NINE

Captivity, even in a tropical paradise, was rotting his brain. Jackson lay perfectly still in the sparse grass, holding a string in his left hand. In front of him, about ten feet away, was a box trap he'd fashioned out of sticks and more string. A little farther out, about twelve feet away, was a blue-and-green lizard, otherwise known as snake bait.

She hadn't said anything about trapping their mysterious visitor. She'd only said he couldn't kill it. Before he could trap the snake, though, he had to trap the bait. Inside the box, he'd staked out a cockroach. All he had to do was wait for Mother Nature to take a ride on the food chain.

A flash of color in the lush growth of forest caught his eye. He glanced up in time to see Sugar disappear behind the base of a gracefully buttressed tree, a splash of bright yellow against a world of unremitting green. Lianas trailed from the higher limbs of the châtaignier, any one of which could be camouflaging the snake he was trying to catch.

He swore under his breath. She was a great one to go forbidding him to do things. He should have forbidden her to go into the forest.

The slightest skittering sound brought his attention back to the lizard, and with a quick jerk of the string, he had his bait trapped in the box, happily eating its last meal.

Now to go get Sugar before something else did.

Sugar carefully picked her way across the rocks at the base of the tiered waterfall that dropped down off the cliffs. Getting to her hideaway was never easy, but it was always worthwhile. She had discovered the small beach and cove while exploring the labyrinth of caverns that honeycombed the cliffs.

Chemical warfare was as prevalent in the rock structure of Cocorico as it was in the forest vegetation. Rain became a diluted carbonic-acid solution by picking up carbon dioxide in the air and from the decomposing plants on the ground. The weak acid dissolved the almost pure calcium carbonate that made up the limestone, sinking through fissures and crannies in the rock to carve out caves over the millennia.

The waterfall was nothing more than a trickle of the river that ran through the caves, four tributaries that had been diverted by breaks high in the outside wall. Far back in the labyrinth, she'd built one of the deeper, more isolated caverns into a water storage tank as a precaution against drought. Once a week she opened the sluice gates on the natural tank and let it empty and refill with fresh water from the river.

She would do that job today, she decided, for she doubted she would get another chance to sneak away. Both men had been preoccupied when she'd come out of the cottage, Jen doing what he spent most of his days doing—looking out to sea—and Jackson sleeping in the grass. That wasn't such an unusual pastime, considering that he spent much of his nights doing what Jen did during the day, but a very unusual pastime for someone worried about big snakes.

A grin twitched her lips. Maybe enamored or challenged was a better way to describe his interest. One animal worthy of the term *dangerous* showed up, and Jackson's protective and predatory instincts rushed to the fore—until the warm sun and soft grass got the better of him.

Still grinning, she reached for the handhold she'd carved in the cliff wall and stepped behind the waterfall.

Sugar disappeared. Jackson stared for a moment at the place where she'd been, then broke into a run, legs pumping, his feet flying through the forest. He vaulted over downed trees and pushed aside branches, heedless of any damage he might do to her plants, though he knew there would be hell to pay when she noticed. He was not going to lose her. She was leading him to freedom. His pulse quickened in anticipation. He'd known there was a way off the island, but he'd be damned if he could find it. Shulan, Sher Chang, and the pilot had left. Henry had left. In a few hours he would leave too.

Or maybe he wouldn't, he thought, even as he leaped to the top of a boulder and jumped down the other side. Not in a few hours anyway. He had time before Shulan returned. Knowing he could escape was the important thing, not the escape itself.

Fool. The warning voice rang loud and clear in his mind and stopped him in his tracks. What in the hell was he thinking?

He grimaced at his faulty, lust-induced reasoning, not believing the direction his thoughts had taken. He needed to leave at the first opportunity, no discussion. He could come back if he found he couldn't live without her, which he sincerely hoped he wouldn't. She was a piece of loose karma, not his destiny. She was a temptation to be overcome, not one to render him helpless. In the worst of scenarios, she wasn't even real, merely a figment of his imagination conjured up by Shulan to tease and entice him, a means to his destruction by the slow, sweet torture of constant arousal and sexual frustration.

Swearing, he scrambled over the last stretch of rocks leading to the source of the stream. The waterfall foamed down in front of him, sending a freshwater mist into the air and obscuring her escape hatch. He stuck his hand through the water and felt rock. He was going after her, and when he found the route to freedom, he was taking it. Twice more he jammed his hand into the water and hit rock, then victory. His arm went through to emptiness, and he followed, cutting through the water and entering another world, one of steaming mist and faint light.

He used both hands to slick his wet hair back off his face. The walls and floor of the cavern were dripping with moisture and covered with an amazing orange-brown slime. There was no sign of Sugar or her passing. He stepped forward, hoping to get a glimpse of her farther back in the cave, but his foot never hit the floor again. There was no floor, only a gaping hole full of mirror-smooth water with his foot breaking the surface. He had enough presence of mind to fill his lungs with air before he went down, flailing for a handhold on the slimy rock, which offered none.

Time ceased to exist under the water. All physical movement dropped into slow motion, except for the pounding of his heart, which jumped into double time as the current sucked him deeper into the hole, into darkness, pulling him down while every survival instinct he had was screaming for him to go up, to regain the surface and life-giving air.

He was scraped against a blunt edge of rock in his headlong flight, but in the middle of the maelstrom there were no surrounding walls, just fast-running water bearing him along. He reached a hand for the surface and encountered a submerged ceiling of solid rock.

True panic set in.

This then was how he was going to die, not as the scornful paramour of the Dragon Whore, nor as the conquering hero of childhood dreams, rescuing fair maidens and dark-eyed beauties, righting injustice and defending the weak, but drowning alone in the dark.

The epitaph no sooner formed than it was disproved. His head came out of the water just as the last of his breath gave way. Lungs burning, he swallowed a gulp of air, then another. His chest heaved with the exertion of trying to catch his breath and keep upright in the swiftly swirling water.

Surrounded by darkness, he fought disorientation by peering into the gloom and using his other senses to fix his location. The sound of rushing water filled his ears. The smell of sweet water overlaid the mustiness in the air, and all around him there was water and more water. He couldn't feel a bottom and keep his head above the river at the same time, and he was disinclined to submerge himself again. There was no telling where he might come up, or what he might come up against.

The current rushed along, propelling him into more darkness, heading deeper and deeper into the earth. Cooper had always said impulsiveness would be the death of him, but the impulse to follow Sugar had been undeniable, instinctive, like a cat chasing a mouse. She'd been running away, and he'd felt a compelling need to chase her. He couldn't have resisted it any more than he could have resisted kissing her.

The river slowed suddenly, as if hitting an invisible wall, and he floated out into a much larger body of water. Ahead of him, across a distance he couldn't estimate, a narrow circle of bright light beckoned.

He began swimming toward the light, controlling each breaststroke so it barely made a ripple. He didn't know where he was or what he might encounter. It was a sure bet Sugar hadn't gone the same way he had, through a hole in the floor. This was her lair, and he'd been caught but good. He just hoped there was another way out. Backtracking his route was out of the question.

He slid through the water, his breath easing back down to normal. Now that death was off the list of imminent possibilities, he was intrigued. The cavern was huge, the ceiling far above him and rustling with movement and noise. If worse came to worst, he wondered if he could eat a bat. He doubted it.

The circle of light grew bigger and brighter, until he could see blue sky and a fringe of greenery around the perimeter. The smell of fresh and growing things cut through the mustiness in the cave. A cloud scudded across the opening. When it passed, a shaft of sunlight pierced the gloom, reaching far into the cavern and reflecting off the sleek form and tangled blond curls of Sugar Caine as she swam silently through the dark pool.

Jackson stopped and treaded water, watching as she reached the opening and pulled herself up onto the ledge. She slicked her hair off her face, shook the water onto the floor, then proceeded to take off her clothes.

A dark thrill shot through him like a streak of wildfire, igniting his mind and body with equal intensity. A nice man would have said something to warn her she wasn't alone. Jackson just watched, a sinful smile curving across his face.

Her T-shirt came off first, skimmed over her head and off her arms, her every move as graceful as a gazelle's. Sunlight lovingly backlit the gentle curves of her body and made a halo around her angel's face.

God, she was beautiful, her breasts small, but full

and round and tipped in pink. He swallowed softly, unable to take his eyes off her.

He followed the descent of her shorts and underwear, his body hardening with every inch of skin she revealed in the wake of the yellow cotton. His smile was long gone. She bent over to pull the clothes off her feet, and when she straightened, his gaze went unerringly to the juncture of her thighs. His tongue came out to dampen suddenly dry lips. He'd seen naked women before, but he hadn't seen Sugar, and something about her made it feel like the first time, the first time for everything. The first time he'd watched a woman undress . . . the first time a woman had opened herself for him . . . the first time he'd slid his hand, and his mouth, and his sex into that magical place.

She raised her arms over her head and stretched from the tips of her fingers to the tips of her toes, and he almost drowned for the second time.

He was entranced. With a powerful kick, he pushed through the water, counting on himself to have enough strength and decency to ask if she'd like to make love before he took her. Then she turned, showing him a luscious backside. That distracted him for the only instant he had to call out and keep her from soaring off the cliff and out of sight.

Watching her fly off the edge cut through his sexual haze pretty damn quick. Five strong strokes brought him to the rocks where she'd left her clothes. He pulled himself up and ran toward the edge, catching himself just before he would have gone over.

A grin broke across his face as he regained his balance. She was already surfacing in the protected cove not ten feet below where he stood, a fair-skinned mermaid in a pool of cerulean blue frothed to white on the edges. He should have known she wasn't the type to take a swan dive. Hell, he hadn't been that much trouble. Not yet, anyway.

Without fear to sidetrack him, his thoughts returned to the more pleasant subject of her nudity and what he was going to do about it. *Take advantage* were the only words that came to mind.

He stripped off his shirt and pulled the drawstring on his pants.

Sugar swam a couple of yards and rolled onto her back to float in the sunshine, but any thoughts she'd had of relaxing in that position were shot to hell when she looked up and saw Jackson. He was poised to dive into the pool, primeval man incarnate, standing tall and strong on the edge of the cliff, a dragon gracing one side of his chest, his long black braid the other. His arms were outstretched, his legs straight, his body as naked as the day he was born.

While a part of her was breathlessly mesmerized, another part of her didn't know how he survived in polite society, or even impolite society.

She did know the only way he could have gotten into her pool, and that made her grin. The bounty hunter's heart was probably still pounding from the wild ride through the sinkhole. Served him right for playing possum, she thought. When she'd passed him in the grass, she could have sworn he was sound asleep.

He pushed off the rocks into a dive, giving her no

more time to contemplate either his body or his motives. Her fight-or-flight instincts kicked into high gear. She chose flight, beating a hasty retreat to the stretch of sand carved out of the thick, overhanging forest that made up most of her hideaway.

When Jackson surfaced, he was alone in the water. Damn. The woman was like quicksilver, impossible to hold. He scanned the cove and finally caught a glimpse of her making her way through the trees. A path led from the southern shore of the pool, winding up the cliff to the opening in the rock wall.

This was the real wild paradise on her island, a deep jungle of green life tied together by miles of lianas and nearly enclosed by the surrounding limestone. Tree roots grew like writhing snakes down the cliff wall, while vines climbed to the arch above. All the flora was heavy with fruit and flowers, filling the cove with splashes of color.

A flock of scarlet macaws with an albino leading the way flew across the pool and swooped up into the trees, squawking noisily. He'd never seen an albino macaw. He doubted if anyone had, except for God, and Sugar, and now him.

Behind him, the ocean waves broke against the reef, sending only a ripple of their strength into the pool. He lowered his head and filled his mouth with water, then spat it back out. The cove was half-fresh, half-salt, a mixture of two great sources of life made out of the same element. Sun, moon; light, dark; yang, yin; man, woman. His woman, and he could not hold on to her.

He saw her hand reach out from behind a small tree

and grab for her clothes. The shirt and shorts were a brilliant shade of yellow, and what with all the fluttering around she did to maintain her modesty behind the tree, she looked like a monarch butterfly.

"Are you decent?" he hollered, still treading water in the middle of the pool.

"Unlike some people I know, I'm always decent," she yelled back from her hiding place, making him smile.

When Jackson didn't respond to her gibe, Sugar stepped closer to the soursop tree and moved aside a leafy branch, only to find he'd disappeared. She watched the water for a long time, her curiosity losing ground to worry with each passing second. The man had said he was a good swimmer. Lord, if he couldn't even manage the cove, how had he expected to catch the *Mary Sue*?

Concern made her careless, and she pressed too closely into the tree, scratching herself on its spiny fruit. She quickly stuck her hand into her mouth and sucked. The faint taste of blood registered on her senses as she again searched the pool.

Her patience and her caution came to an end at the same time. She readied herself to dive in after him, ducking under the tree's lowest branch and stepping to the edge. What stopped her was the sight of him climbing up the cliff wall at her feet, hand over fist, using a thick liana as a rope and tree roots for footholds.

He moved with the agility of an animal in its prime, scaling the cliff with purposeful ease. Water and sunlight glistened over his tawny skin and down the free-falling corded braid of his hair. When he reached the top, he looked up at her with a mischievous gleam in his eye.

"Me Jackson. You Sugar," he said, sounding innocent and looking dangerously sensual, his smile guileless but not harmless.

For an instant she was sucked into the fantasy he offered—one man, one woman, no rules—but only for an instant.

"Me going. You nuts," she said, backing away from the edge.

"Give me a hand up?" he asked, and she stopped in midstep. He raised one hand toward her, and she couldn't help but notice what that did to the muscles in the arm holding on to the vine. They tightened, becoming even more well defined.

He couldn't possibly need help, not with arms like his, but she stepped forward out of a sense of duty. She offered him her hand, and immediately regretted it.

He took hold of her hand and pulled at the same time as he pushed off from the rock wall, sending them both out over the water. Sugar instinctively stretched her body into a dive position, and he did the same, but he didn't let go of her. When they surfaced, she spluttering and he grinning, he still had hold of her.

"You—you got me wet!" She would have called him something awful, but he defied description.

"You were already wet," he said, his smile broadening in a flash of white teeth.

"I was halfway dry." It was a bit of a stretch, but close enough. "And I could have been hurt with you dragging me off the cliff like that."

He laughed. "Halfway dry is about as good as it gets on Cocorico, and I held on to you so you wouldn't get hurt." He clearly wasn't taking the blame for anything. He began swimming toward the shore, pulling her beside him.

"You can . . . uh, let go of me now."

"No, I can't," he said, cutting through the blue-green water, his movements sending tiny waves lapping against her throat and chest.

"Why not?"

"Because the only reason I pulled you off the cliff was so I could hold you." He found his footing on the bottom and drew her into his embrace within the shadows of the overhanging palms. "After going to that much trouble, it would be a shame not to take full advantage of the opportunity."

She wanted to disagree, despite what her heart felt was the truth. Yes, it would be a shame to waste such a golden opportunity for holding each other, but being that close to him in broad daylight made speech impossible. Her pulse was beating too quickly, and her thoughts were moving too slowly.

His mouth was so beautiful, wide set with lips softer than they looked, and teeth so white they fairly shone against the darker color of his skin. A woman would give up a lot to explore a mouth like his, especially when the woman already knew what sensory magic he could conjure with his kiss.

"Sugar?" He spoke her name softly, his voice husky with the changing tension in the air.

She lifted her gaze to meet his and felt an ache build

inside her chest. His mouth was no more beautiful than his eyes. Or his hair. Or his body.

Or his warrior's heart with its tenderness and easy laughter. She couldn't resist him forever. She could only give him fair warning of the truth.

Nervously wetting her lips, she forced herself not to falter under the weight of her words.

"If you kiss me again, Jackson, I swear I'll never let you go." Her lashes lowered before the last word was out, a minor concession considering what she'd just confessed.

He was quiet for a long time, holding her against him, the gentle rise and fall of his chest the only movement she could perceive.

"Do you mean that?" he finally asked, his voice full of the hundred other questions he hadn't asked.

She nodded, afraid to say more.

"You're thinking about letting me go?" He didn't sound as if he believed it, but she wasn't going to reassure him with even à gesture. She'd already given away too much.

"But not if I kiss you," he repeated, then swore roundly, his hands tightening on her waist. "Somebody should have taught you when to cut your losses. I can't—"

Whatever he was going to say next was lost in the drone of a low-flying seaplane banking into the point, headed for the beach below her home.

He swore again, a word much nastier than her own vehement damn.

"Looks like somebody has saved you again," he said, not sounding any too happy about it.

"What do you mean?" She didn't feel saved, she felt invaded. No one was scheduled to come. Shulan had told her three weeks.

"What I mean"—he captured her chin and turned her face up to meet his glowering gaze—"is that you have *greatly* underestimated how much you mean to me."

His mouth came down on hers hard and forceful, demanding a response she was incapable of hiding.

Jackson cursed himself again and again, even as he sank deeper into the kiss, into the taste and feel of Sugar Caine, the woman who would be his doom.

TEN

He was lost, more lost than he'd been in Shulan's gilded Hong Kong prison. There, it had only been his body in a strange place. On Cocorico, with Sugar in his arms, he was racing down uncharted paths of the heart.

He lifted his head to place another kiss on her lips, loving the luxury of being able to leave and come back for more. There were no tears this time. She was as fascinated as he was with the sweet melding of their mouths.

When next he lifted his head and looked, her wide gray eyes were dazed with passion, her cheeks flushed with color. Relief and satisfaction filled his breast. Sometimes she tried too hard to be indifferent to him, coolly in control, and he didn't want her cool where he was concerned. He couldn't have borne her manufactured indifference, not when he was drowning in a whirlpool of emotion.

Holding her face in his hands, he kissed her again,

simply pressing his lips to hers and breathing in the same air. She was his woman, like no other woman, made for him to be hers.

The sound of the plane engine ended abruptly, warning him it had landed on the other side of the arch. If they'd come to take him, they were going to be disappointed. He wasn't going anywhere.

"Stay with me," he said roughly, kissing her ear, her temple, her brow.

"I can't stay here, Jackson, and neither can you." She tilted her head back, away from his roaming mouth. Her expression was serious despite the flush still suffusing her cheeks and the lambent light in her eyes. "They may not have seen us, but they know about this cove. They'll search every inch of the island until they find you, unless I throw them off your track."

"Do they know about the caves?"

"No, but the seaplane will give them access to this place. You can't stay here."

A hint of desperation shaded her voice, taking away its soft lilt and impressing upon him the depth of her feelings for him. Either she'd been telling the truth and she wasn't going to let him go—or let anyone take him —because he'd kissed her, or her concern for him had suddenly won out over any loyalty she felt she owed Shulan. He considered the change good joss, regardless of her motives.

"What will you tell them?" he asked, deliberately not using Shulan's name. She had just committed herself to a breach of faith with her friend, choosing him over the pirate princess. He didn't want to press the point.

"That I took you to another island."

"Why?" He spoke with the obvious inflection of an interrogator, giving her a chance to get her story straight.

"Because I didn't feel you were safe here any longer."

He shot another question at her. "Why?"

"Because the security of the island was breached."

"How?"

"An unauthorized boat landing."

"When?"

"Two nights ago."

"Who was it?"

"I'm not sure. They . . . uh, said they were—had gotten blown off course," she said, struggling to keep up the lie. "But they didn't look like run-of-the-mill windjamming tourists."

"Why not? What was different about them?"

"I don't know," she said, throwing her hands up, exasperated. "They were just different, that's all."

"You're not a very good liar, Sugar," he said straight out.

"That's not what you thought a few days ago." Her smile was faintly wry.

He answered her with a smile of his own. "A few days ago I didn't know I was in love."

It was a hell of a bombshell to drop, and she wasn't any more surprised than he was by the declaration. He hadn't meant to say it, he hadn't thought to say it. He'd just said it.

"That's impossible," she whispered, her eyes growing wide. It wasn't exactly the response he would have put at the top of his most wanted list.

"Yeah, well, a lot of impossible things seem to happen here." He felt color rise in his cheeks, at least that's what he thought he felt. He couldn't remember ever blushing before.

"You're blushing," she confirmed, her smile teasing him to the point that he lowered his gaze—for all of a second and a half. He liked being teased by her too much to miss a moment of it.

"Let that be our first secret," he said. "Cooper will never let me live it down, if he ever finds out."

"I've never been any good at keeping secrets, but I promise to keep yours." Her voice softened along with the look in her eyes, reminding him again of the fierceness of her convictions. The few things she had to hold on to, she held on to with a tenacious and sincere loyalty.

"Our secret," he corrected her, running his thumb across her bottom lip. He'd been right to follow her, though the freedom she was leading him to was far different from what he'd expected. "So what are you going to tell them?"

"The truth," she said. "Or as close to the truth as I can get. That you were driving me absolutely crazy and I had to get rid of you. That you wouldn't keep your clothes on and you wouldn't stay out of the water. That you upset my schedule and unearthed snakes in the garden. That I couldn't think a coherent thought when you were near me."

"Are you in love too?" It was the hardest question he'd ever asked, and her answer wasn't nearly what he'd hoped it would be.

"I don't know, Jackson," she said, being painfully honest. "I want you so much, I can't see beyond the wanting. You're more than I ever expected to get."

"More what?"

"More life, more of a chance."

Her answer hurt him worse than her doubts about love. She was too young to have settled for so little.

"There must have been a time when your dreams were bigger, Sugar."

"Maybe," she said, her lashes lowering for a moment. Then she turned away from him. "I'm sorry. We have to go now, before they come looking."

He stopped her from leaving by laying his hand on her arm, but she didn't look at him. "You can't hide from me forever."

When she didn't answer, he let her go. He couldn't hold her with force, and he wasn't going to get answers by asking questions, not yet, though he was damned determined to get some answers. His love gave him a right to know everything about her, an obligation.

Patience would bring him her trust, he told himself, and only trust would give him the secrets of her past—or a chance at her future. Patience.

He followed her up the narrow trail leading to the opening of the cavern. The path was sandy, easy on bare feet, when it should have been rocky. With little effort, he could imagine her spending days hauling sand up from the beach to pack the trail, making her walled paradise more amenable, adding a small luxury to her life.

Her island was beautiful, lush, and giving, but it was still a prison. If not his love, he wondered what it would take to lure her from her Eden. And if she didn't love him in return, did he have any right to ask her to leave?

At the top of the path, she waited with her back to him while he put on his clothes.

"We don't have to go back the way we came in, do we?" he asked, pulling his pants on before reaching for his T-shirt.

"You don't, but I would rather go back the way I came in," she said.

Her meaning wasn't lost on him.

"I knew you didn't come through that sinkhole." He was relieved he'd been right, more for her sake than his own. He was big enough to take a little knocking around.

"I did the first time," she said, effectively dispelling his relief. "As I remember, it was quite a ride."

He stopped with his shirt halfway on. The vision he had of her being taken by surprise and sucked down into the watery darkness chilled him to the core. With a deft move, he pulled the shirt over his head. Anything could happen to her at any time, and no one would know, maybe not forever.

"Yeah, it was quite a ride," he agreed, making up his mind. He was leaving, and when he left, she was going with him. If Cooper hadn't already neutralized Baolian, he would, doing whatever it took to get the Dragon Whore off Sugar's back.

"Sinkhole on your left," Sugar warned, leading Jackson through a wide tunnel. They'd already passed her storage tank and replaced the sluice gates at the top. He'd been impressed with her ingenuity. Sugar barely noticed. She was still stunned by his declaration of love.

He wasn't in love, of course. Lust, maybe, but not love. Love took time, and they'd had none to speak of, nor were they likely to get any. He deserved to have control of his life without any more interference from Shulan, and she was going to make sure he got it. After Shulan left, she would take him to Kingstown and set him free. If he'd truly been injured and in need of rest and care, what Shulan had asked of her wouldn't have been as difficult or as distasteful. Under the circumstances, though, she'd held him longer than she should have. It was time to let him go.

She stiffened her resolve to keep from feeling horrible. It was the damn "love" thing. He never should have said those words. They made her guilt unbearable. The thought of being alone again was even worse.

He'd ruined her peace of mind, and her peace of body. She didn't know about love, but she knew she felt lust. She had felt it from the first moment she'd laid eyes on him, so gloriously naked, stretched out on her bed.

She also knew better than to confuse a sexual response with love, and under normal circumstances, he probably did too. She'd heard there was often an attraction between a captive and his captor, a hostage syndrome. She didn't doubt that what he was experiencing was a mixture of lust and hostage syndrome.

The realization made her feel completely pathetic.

"I don't know how you ever got through these caves the first time without getting killed," he said. "Or what in the hell you were doing in here to begin with."

"I was careful," she said, "and I didn't have a choice about being in here. Once I fell through the first sinkhole behind the waterfall and ended up at the cove, I had to find a way out." She shot the beam of her flashlight on a jagged protrusion of limestone. "Watch yourself on the wall here. It's like a razor."

The flashlight was one that never left the caves. She kept it in a waterproof box at the entrance to the tunnel that led from the waterfall to the cavern that emptied out into the cove. At the cove end of the tunnel was another plastic box to store it in before she went for her swim. A spare set of batteries was always taped to the flashlight. She'd mapped the caves and tunnels and sinkholes, but without a light to guide her, she would be as lost and in danger as she'd been the first time—and she'd vowed never to be caught that unprepared again.

She heard him swear behind her.

"What?" she asked, swinging the light around on him.

"I think I jigged when I should have jagged." His voice was tight. The flashlight showed him inspecting a diagonal line of blood on his biceps.

She rushed back to him. "Dammit. I'm sorry." She

touched him, running her fingers down the smooth skin of his arm, checking him over. "I don't think it's very deep."

"It's not," he said through clenched teeth.

"More of a scratch than a cut." She tried to reassure him, but sensed her failure in the tension radiating off him.

"Yeah, just a scratch." He bent his head over hers, trapping her within an invisible cocoon of strained intimacy. He started to speak, then caught himself.

"What's the matter, Jackson? Are you in pain?" She let her concern show in the tenderness of her touch and the softness of her voice.

"No, I— Do you do that a lot, Sugar?" he blurted out. "Walk around falling into sinkholes and getting 'maytagged' in underwater tunnels?"

"No," she said, relieved he was only worried about her and not hurt worse than she'd thought.

"How long did it take you to find your way out of here?" His tone didn't leave much room for a lie, though considering his mood, a lie would have been preferable to the truth.

"Two days," she confessed, then added, "give or take a few hours."

She should have lied.

"Two days?" he repeated, sounding both angry and incredulous. "Two damn days down here? You must have been scared senseless."

She gave a short laugh. "I've only been scared senseless once, and believe me, Jackson, that wasn't it."

Her offhand statement proved to be another tactical error.

"Having experienced both," he said, his voice lowering to a ragged whisper, "the only thing I can imagine that would be worse than being trapped down here and not knowing where I was, would be standing in front of Fang Baolian without a gun in my hand."

The man was uncanny.

"I had a knife," she admitted, feeling she owed him something, an explanation or part of the truth. He already knew more about her than was safe. A little more information wouldn't make any difference—except possibly in the way he remembered her.

Regardless, the instant the words were out of her mouth, she regretted them. Even in the poor illumination of the flashlight she saw his face harden.

"A knife?" The words hung in the air, disbelieving. "What the hell kind of knife were you carrying? Balisong? Tanto? Kriss? Buck?"

"Steak."

"A steak knife?"

"I took it off the buffet. It was a New Year's Eve party. Things got out of hand."

Jackson had wanted to know. He'd practically forced her into telling him, only to find out she'd tangled with the Dragon Whore *mano a mano?*

He wanted to strip her down and look for the scars. Nobody got that close to Baolian, not with deadly intent, without feeling the sting of her scorpion's nails, the razor-edged blades that tipped each of her fingers.

"How in the ever-lovin' hell did you end up at a

New Year's Eve party with the likes of Fang Baolian?" He stared at her, dumbfounded.

"I went with some friends."

"Where?" he asked incredulously. "Some opium den in Manila? A flophouse in Jakarta? A gutter in Hong Kong?"

"A mansion on Mustique."

He'd heard of the Caribbean island, a high-priced sanctuary for millionaires and rock-and-roll stars, and apparently at least one international crime queen.

"Did you cut her?" he asked, then waved the question away. "Forget it. You must have cut her or you wouldn't have ended up in exile here for— How long, Sugar?"

"Three years."

Jackson felt as if someone had punched him in the solar plexus. Three years? She'd been there for three years? In a flash, he thought back to all he'd done in the last three years, the places he'd been, the people he'd met, the things he'd done—the things he shouldn't have done.

"No," he said, shaking his head and disbelieving every word she'd told him. "I've seen the woman, most if not all of her, and there wasn't a mark on her worth three years of your life."

"She thought differently at the time," Sugar said, fighting an unwelcome surge of jealousy. "I'm sure she still does." She remembered how Baolian had looked three years ago, sinfully seductive, beautiful and powerful, her skin flawless, like the finest porcelain—and he had seen the woman practically naked.

"What friends were you with?" He lifted both of his hands in a gesture of confusion. "Baolian has no friends. Not one. She is not a party-type girl. She does business, that's all. Business to make money."

"Is that what she was doing with you? Making money?" The question came out snooty and accusing, and just reeking with the old green-eyed monster.

A long silence drew out between them and ended with a quirk of his eyebrow. "If you believe Shulan's story, yes. Personally, I think she was after my body."

He was so cool, so matter-of-fact, she wanted to shake him. Of course the woman had been after his body. What woman in her right mind wouldn't be after his body?

"These friends of yours, Sugar," he said, getting back to the subject at hand. "What happened to them? Why are you the only one here?" He wasn't asking nicely, far from it. He sounded like he wanted to take names for future reference.

"They were just friends, casual friends," she said to disarm him. Not that she was going to give him names. Their names meant nothing. "They were in the islands for the Christmas holiday, most of them richer and all of them wilder than me. Somebody knew somebody on Mustique, and they got us an invitation. I thought the party would be fun. I was wrong, and I got into trouble." The pained look he was giving her put her on the defensive. "These things do happen, you know, especially when you're young and you're so damn sure that living for the moment is the only sensible thing to do."

Jackson silently agreed. Having spent a good portion of his life getting into trouble, he knew exactly how those things happened, how easy trouble was to find. Most times it was just lying there in the middle of whatever road he was on, waiting for him to step into the snare.

"You're still young," he said, squelching the urge to lecture her about the dangers of moving with a fast crowd. She was already paying the price. "And you're still too damn sure of everything."

"Not like I was." He heard no regret in her voice. She said it like a person who had learned something the hard way.

He watched her through the steamy mist filling the air and dampening their bodies. He had enough regrets for both of them, for the years she'd lost. He was beginning to understand why she was such a fascinating, frustrating blend of woman and child. She'd been alone far longer than he would have believed possible, missing all the opportunities given youth to make the transition to full adulthood.

The noise of running water echoed through the tunnels, sounding like a thousand rivers under the earth. The flashlight beam caught in the mists, reflecting off the vapor and casting shadows on the floor, the whole adding a haze of unreality to everything around them. Her pale hair and yellow clothes gave her even less substance, made her seem more of an angel than a woman, and he wanted her to be a woman. He didn't want her to slip away from him again.

With a heavy sigh, she shifted her gaze, dragging her hand back through her hair.

"We're fighting again," she said, her voice tinged with a hint of weariness.

"I know." He reached out and tilted her face up, needing to touch her and reconfirm the life and warmth of her. Getting angry wasn't getting him anywhere.

He smoothed the pad of his thumb over her skin, following the curve from her brow to her ear. She was lovely, fresh and exotic, utterly female, and she was supposed to be his. He would, and probably was, betting his life on that fact, but she needed convincing.

"There's an old Chinese saying," he said, "about riding the dragon through gates of jade to cool its burning fire."

She gave him a quizzical glance. "And what in the world does that mean?"

"If we make love, we'll stop fighting." He let a slow, easy grin curve his mouth.

She lowered her lashes and fiddled with the hem of her shirt, looking uncharacteristically flustered. "You make it sound like a prescription cure."

"For what's been bothering you and me, it is. We could use some practice in getting along and working as a team, and good sex takes a lot of getting along and teamwork." He bent his head and tried to glimpse her face. "It's a helluva lot more fun than hockey, Sugar. Or basketball. Think of it as an adventure. You explore me, I explore you, and we share the treasure." Sounded good to him.

Instead of returning his smile as he'd hoped, she looked away, off into the darkness of the tunnel behind them. She'd twisted her shirt into a knot at the bottom.

"That night on Mustique, one of the friends, a boy, wasn't so casual."

His teasing mood instantly vanished. He didn't want to hear this.

"He was a couple of years older than me and I'd known him just long enough to convince myself I was in love," she went on, really making him wish she would stop. "He'd hardly been on St. Vincent a week before we were talking marriage. I know that sounds dumb."

His heart sank. He didn't think it sounded dumb. Hell, he hadn't been with her even a week and he was thinking in long terms himself.

"What happened?" he asked, hoping to bypass the more intimate details. She was his, should have been his from the very beginning.

"We went to the party with all his friends. They chartered a plane and everything, champagne and caviar, probably drugs. I don't know. I was pretty naive." A breeze snaked through the tunnel, stirring the tendrils of steam. "Come on," she said. "We better keep moving."

She stepped around a corner, and he followed. "What happened at the party?"

"Corey, that was the boy, got drunk. I think he was drunk even before we got off the plane. Sinkhole." She flashed the light on the floor to warn him. "There must have been a hundred people at the estate. It was like a lot of different little parties going on all over the house and grounds. Corey wandered into one he shouldn't have."

"And you followed him." It was a simple statement

and not the question he wanted to ask, which was about the kind of friends she'd had who would invite Fang Baolian to a damn New Year's Eve party.

"The people were older, more formal. I'm not even sure it was a party. There were a lot of servants. At least that's what I thought at the time. Later I realized they were guards or soldiers. Anyway, the room was crawling with them and they were all kowtowing to this beautiful Asian lady dressed in black."

Baolian, Jackson thought. She was the quintessential woman in black. No one did the look better, or with such deadly grace.

"I could tell right off that we didn't belong there, but Corey was too drunk and too arrogant to think there might be anyplace he didn't belong. I think his dad was a politician or something, maybe a senator."

All around them, the sound of running water was getting louder, and he wondered if they were nearing the waterfall. Then he realized the water wasn't ahead of them, it was above them. He instinctively ducked and swore under his breath, as if either one of those defense mechanisms would save them if the roof caved in.

"He couldn't take his eyes off the Asian lady," Sugar continued, "and when she finally noticed him, the attraction was obviously mutual."

"Baolian does have a thing for younger men," he said, knowing the truth only too well. The woman had a good twenty years on him.

He looked up at the roof again, eyeing it warily. Cooper would never top this one.

"Well, her taste has improved since then," Sugar

said. She took the end of her shirt and wiped some of the dampness off her face. "We're in for a little geothermal action up ahead. The water gets really hot. Be careful."

"Right," he said, already feeling the heat. "So what happened after love at first sight?"

Her laugh was bitter. "I should have been grateful Baolian saved me from getting any more . . . uh, involved with Corey, heartless jerk that he turned out to be. But at the time I was too crushed, and all I wanted to do was get out of there. Some guy thought differently, though. I avoided him for a while, thinking Corey would come to his senses, walk away from this woman in black, and we would leave together, but it didn't work out that way."

"You wouldn't happen to remember the guy's name, would you?" He told himself it was a professional question—anyone who partied with Fang Baolian had to be up to no good—but he was lying. He wanted the man's name for personal reasons.

"No," she said. "We didn't get to introductions. We did end up in a strange room. I thought I'd been working my way out of the house, but I was actually getting in deeper. The room was all mirrors and silk, everything in red, yellow, and black, and there was even a feast laid out on a table. There was music playing, candles and incense burning. Before I could get back out of the room, the guy grabbed me. I grabbed a knife."

Sugar paused. "I didn't mean to cut her. I didn't even know she and Corey were in the room, until I stumbled over them. They were lying on these pillows and they were . . . Anyhow, I stumbled over them, tried to catch myself, and that's when the knife cut her."

"Where did you cut her?" He had seen more of Baolian than he'd ever wanted to see, and for the life of him, he couldn't remember any knife scars.

Sugar looked over her shoulder at him and a teasing glint came into her eyes. "Right across the biscuits, cheek to cheek. I think she would have killed me on the spot, but with all the blood and screaming, I had a couple seconds' lead. She still would have had me if someone hadn't pulled me into a hidden passageway. From there I was able to get back to the plane. I laid low in the baggage compartment until it took off."

They ducked under a smooth arch, and Jackson could have sworn it was getting lighter in the tunnels.

"So that explains Baolian," he said. "How did you get involved with Shulan?"

"She was the one who grabbed me when I was running. We'd gone to the same private school on Barbados. She was a few years behind me. We all knew she was rich, living off a trust fund in the Caymans, but I didn't know her mother was the Dragon Queen of the South China Sea, or that she spent her vacations on Mustique. None of us did. After I got back to St. Vincent, I toughed it out for a few months—"

"Toughed what out?"

She shrugged. "Things started happening."

"Things? What kind of things?" It was definitely getting lighter and warmer.

"Bad things. My cat and dog were killed, innocent

people were hurt, crippled in a car bomb meant for me, people I loved."

He swore silently. Those were mean games to get caught in.

"I thought that was too high a price for one girl's dubious honor. I went back to Shulan, begged her to intercede with her mother, to tell her I would do anything."

"Baolian doesn't work that way," he said, controlling his anger. No one in Baolian's position worked that way. He'd met all types of pirates over the years, and as far as he could tell, only the ruthless had a chance in hell of surviving to rob and plunder another day.

"That's what Shulan told me. The best she could do, she said, was to help me disappear until her mother forgot me. I ended up here. Shulan owns the island, but I've got a ninety-nine-year lease. She's one of my few regular visitors."

"Who are the others?" he asked.

"Carolina, Henry, sometimes my father. Every now and then, Shulan lets a scientist come to study for a day or two."

"What about your mother?"

A moment of silence preceded her reply. "She comes when she can. It's hard for her." She flipped off the flashlight. "We're here." An opening in the cave's ceiling flooded the cavern with sunshine.

"Where?" he asked, looking around at the slick rock and the column of steam rising out of a pool in the middle of the floor. Most of the steam went out the ceiling hole, but a good portion also drifted into the tunnel they'd left.

"I call it Coeur de Cocorico, the heart of Cocorico," she said. "By the time I come back for you, you'll probably be calling it the sauna from hell. It's the only thing like it on the island. If it gets too unbearable, the waterfall is ten yards that way." She pointed toward one of the smaller tunnels. "The sinkhole you fell in the first time is the only one you have to worry about. There aren't any others in that direction."

He looked up at the circle in the ceiling. Like the one above the secret pool, it was nearly enclosed with greenery. Even here, large tree roots grew down inside the cavern, both holding it together and breaking it apart.

"Isn't it unusual to have a single, isolated spot of geothermal activity?"

She shrugged. "When you live on Cocorico, you learn to accept the mysteries of life."

"Like four-tiered waterfalls and giant snakes, shark alleys and albino scarlet macaws, and rivers that run overhead?"

The laugh he got out of her almost made the whole convoluted mess worthwhile. A kiss would have clinched the deal.

"You forgot the mist," she said. "When you see it, you'll definitely think it's mysterious."

"And you?" he added. She'd held something back in her story. He didn't know what, but he knew the secret held part of the key as to why she'd accepted exile over taking a chance.

"No." She shook her head. "There's no mystery to me. I'll try to come back shortly after nightfall with food. If they leave earlier, I'll come then. Will you be okay?"

No, he didn't think he would be okay, not without her kiss, but he didn't tell her. He showed her, pulling her into his arms and lowering his mouth to hers. For the first time there was no resistance in her. She came to him with parted lips and melted against him, accepting everything he gave, meeting every stroke of his tongue with one of hers, teasing and delighting him with her shy explorations.

The kiss took him back in time, toward the beginning when first breath was given. They were both warm and wet, entwined within the womb of the cave, a fiery caldron at their feet and a clear blue sky above them.

Earth, wind, water, and fire—the alchemist's potions worked their magic and drew him ever deeper into her spell.

ELEVEN

Sugar knew she was in trouble the minute she saw Jen lying in the courtyard, bound hand and foot, surrounded by soldiers. She was still within the protective cover of the forest and turned to flee, but she didn't get more than three feet before the metallic slap of a lowered gun and a barked command stopped her in midflight.

The language was Chinese, but the man's tone gave the words clear meaning: Stop or I'll shoot.

Jackson had never been any good at taking orders or sitting still. He paced the confines of the cave, restless. Their plan made perfect sense, for him to stay and for her to go, but it wasn't setting right. If he'd gone with her, he would have been taken only God knew where in Shulan's misguided attempt to keep her half brother safe. At least that's what the pirate princess kept insisting. It was certainly what Sugar believed. He wasn't so sure.

There was no doubt his father had been Asian. Jackson only had to look down at his skin or his hair to confirm the genetics. A glance in a mirror would reinforce the fact. Except for the color of his eyes and a vaguely prominent bridge in his nose, he was as Asian as chopsticks. But those truths did not mean he was the son of the most notorious pirate to sail the South China Sea, a title surrendered to Fang Baolian only upon Sun Yi's deathbed.

On the other hand, if a person was to cross the pure green of Cooper's eyes with the warm golden amber of Shulan's, they'd end up with Jackson Daniels. It wasn't exactly scientific evidence, but it was something to think about.

He'd rather think about Sugar, the gray-eyed one. He stopped his pacing and ran his hand along one of the thick, exposed tree roots growing down from the opening in the ceiling. A narrowly slanted shaft of sunlight slipped up the cave walls, reminding him of the lateness of the hour. It would be dark soon. Tilting his head back, he looked up into the fading blue sky fringed with a verdant forest, and it beckoned to him.

With a bend of his knees, he jumped up and reached as high as he could, grabbing onto a gnarly curve of root and pulling himself up. He found a foothold against the wall and pushed, straining higher. In a few minutes he'd reached the opening and levered himself over the top and into a bed of sweet-smelling grass. Breathing deeply, he rolled onto his back, spreading his arms out at his sides.

A breeze blew across his face, bringing the scents of flowers and fruit and the ever-present sea. She'd told him what he'd wanted to know, and maybe something more. A grin teased his mouth. He could imagine Baolian's rage at having her curvy little behind scarred for life. She was a woman who prided herself on her beauty as much as her brains and her ruthlessness.

It was impossible to imagine a man loving both the Dragon Whore and Jackson's mother. The woman he remembered from his childhood had been gentle and loving, and afraid most of the time. She'd been too vulnerable to Old Man Daniels's anger and abuse. Baolian, on the other hand, didn't know the meaning of the word *fear*, and the only abuse she dealt in was the abuse she dished out. Together, the two women would have made one good, strong woman. Maybe that had been their appeal to the same man—if the story was true.

He wondered if Cooper knew about Sun Yi. And if his brother did know something, why hadn't he told him? It wasn't like Cooper to hold back information. He'd stopped protecting his little brother from the crueler realities and harder edges of life the day Jackson had delivered a high roundhouse kick and broken his first board during martial-arts training.

If Cooper had known, he would have said something. Shulan had to be wrong. And yet . . . and yet . . .

He rolled onto his stomach and into a patch of diminutive orchids. The blooms were white and blushed with a mauvy green in the center. He slipped his hand through the flowers, gathering them into his palm and crushing them as he brought them to his face. Their scent infused his senses and made him smile. They smelled of Sugar.

She was a virgin. That was the information she'd given but hadn't spoken aloud. A virgin saved by a poorly wielded blade, saved for him. He closed his eyes and inhaled the perfume he'd made with his hand and nature's bounty. He would make love with her, and it would be sweet—to watch her eyes darken, to use slow hands and a teasing tongue to seduce her past inhibitions, to take her body and give her his and let her wonder at the magic they could conjure with a touch.

An angry shout from below knocked him out of his reverie. He was on his feet in a flash and scrambling for the ledge overlooking Sugar's compound. An elephant-ear leaf provided him with the cover he needed to get closer to the edge. He inched forward until he could see, and what he saw froze him in place, except for his mind, which raced at double time trying to come up with enough versions of the word *fool*.

He'd known it wasn't right to send her out alone. The isolation of Cocorico had dulled his instincts for danger. They'd assumed only Shulan would come, but the men in the courtyard were wearing the colors of Fang Baolian's honor guard, black gis and red headbands. They were wushu storm troopers, men trained in every known weapon and in the art of hand-to-hand combat; and they always traveled in groups of nine, a *jiu*, eight fighters and a captain.

Jackson swore vehemently. How could he have let her walk through the waterfall without doing reconnaissance? His instincts weren't dulled, they were friggin' comatose. She'd told him he was at the edge of the world, and he'd started believing it.

Their leader, identified by the double red insignia on the shoulder of his uniform, ducked out from under the bungalow's verandah, and Jackson wondered what great sin he'd committed or which god he'd failed to appease to deserve such bad joss.

Shulan had a traitor in her midst. Sher Chang, six feet four inches and two hundred eighty pounds of mean, shouted a stream of commands in a staccato rhythm, getting everyone moving except for the two people tied back-to-back in the courtyard, Jen and Sugar.

Five of the soldiers fanned out, quartering the area. Sher Chang turned his attention to Sugar, going down on one knee in front of her and cupping her chin in his huge, meaty hand. A lewd smile spread across his round face and sweat glistened on his bald head. Jackson couldn't hear what he said, but Sugar grew whiter with every movement of the bastard's lips. She looked unbelievably small and fragile compared with the giant, and something ugly twisted in Jackson's gut to see her at Sher Chang's mercy. His only consolation was in knowing Baolian's captain would want to use Sugar to bargain with him and was unlikely to damage the goods until the parlay was over.

The brute released her with a rough laugh and a pat

on the cheek, but the son of a bitch had left marks on her face. Those marks sealed his fate.

Jackson scooted out from under the green bower of leaves and made his way back to the opening of the cave. His best chance was to take out the soldiers while they were searching the forest. Catching each one alone improved the odds in his favor, despite the firepower they were packing.

The sun fell lower in the sky with each passing moment, heading toward its nightly immersion into the sea. The last rays of bright light glanced off the face of the arch as he eased himself over the side of the pit and dropped down into darkness.

Sugar was furious with herself. Three years of caution had been blown all to hell with one false assumption: that Shulan, and only Shulan, would have been on the plane, or would have authorized someone else to land at Cocorico. The possibility of Baolian's foul presence had never crossed her mind, not even come close to her consciousness. She'd been so concerned with saving Jackson, she'd forgotten to save herself.

The traitor was Sher Chang, the huge giant who had brought Jackson to the island. But he hadn't come for Jackson. He'd come for her and the bounty promised by Baolian to the man, woman, or child who brought her the silver-eyed whore's head on a platter. Or so he'd told her with his greasy face shoved up next to hers and his fingers nearly breaking her jaw in their grip. Jackson was a mere bonus compared to the grand prize.

The first drops of rain hit as the sun sank into the sea, making its final farewell with a streaking flash of green across the horizon. Tonight was the night of the full moon. There would be light in the sky to illumine the intruders' way, but shadows everywhere to conceal; and fog, thick, rolling banks of it, to disorient and give her a chance to save herself and Jackson.

If in the end there proved to be no chance for escape, she would at least make damn sure someone shot her. After seeing what Baolian had done to her cat and her dog, the horrible cruelty of their deaths, Sugar had sworn never to let the Dragon Queen take her alive. She'd rather die quickly with a bullet or a dozen bullets than be tortured, maimed, mauled, and raped to death.

Sher Chang had promised her all that, and more.

Jackson waited for the light to fail, giving himself the added edge of darkness. The waterfall made a sheet of translucent shifting gray in front of him, while behind him, cool rain fell into the bubbling pool and made billowing clouds of steam. He was sitting with the soles of his feet together and pulled in close to his body, his knees resting on the floor of the cave, his groin muscles softening and stretching, relaxing so he could kick clean and true.

He would make his sweep from west to east, taking down each man in turn. There was no margin for error, and he had neither the time nor the strength to end up on the ground in a grappling match with any of Baolian's guards. Each strike had to be perfectly timed and delivered with power. Each strike had to count.

He stood and bent at the waist, touching his forehead to his legs, keeping his knees straight to stretch the muscles along the backs of his thighs and calves. With his palms touching, he straightened and raised his arms above his head, lengthening his torso by reaching higher and higher. He breathed deeply and evenly, readying himself for battle, slipping far down inside himself to find his warrior's spirit and bring it to the fore.

The only weapons he had were contained within his body. He couldn't afford for it to fail.

The light shimmering through the waterfall dimmed, telling him it was time. There were no choices to be made, therefore no hesitations. He and Sugar had one chance to cheat Baolian out of their deaths, and the chance lay in the strength of his heart. He stepped through the waterfall and into the twilight of the lush forest.

Rain fell from the sky, adding the soothing rhythm of water hitting and running off leaves to the rushing sound of the falls. He made his way down the stream, staying low.

He heard the first man before he saw him, a shadow with substance following the trail up to the falls, and positioned himself for the takedown, molding himself to the trunk of a tree. Surprise was his great advantage. As the man passed, Jackson lashed out with a high kick to the head. The soldier went down without a sound, never knowing what hit him.

Jackson collected his gun and moved on. Cooper would have been proud.

Jen had managed the impossible. Sugar discreetly rubbed her free wrists, then took the tiny blade he'd produced from out of nowhere and began sawing away at his bonds. When he'd first wiggled up against her, she'd thought the old man had picked a hell of a time to make a pass. The language barrier had effectively garbled the message he'd been so intent on hissing and whispering at her, giving her the impression that he was not only making a pass, but that doing it under duress added a certain excitement for him.

She'd been just short of complete disgust and calling out to one of the guards when he'd nicked her. She'd sworn, he'd apologized—she thought—and they'd started working as a team. His timing couldn't have been better. The rain had stopped and tendrils of steamy mist were floating across the ground and hanging in the trees. It would only be minutes before the fog bank began forming out on the open water, pulling cool moisture from the ocean and mixing it with the air. If they could be free of each other by then, they could slip away unseen.

"Whoa, sweet momma." Jackson stopped cold, waving his arms out at his sides to balance himself and to keep from stepping right into the middle of eleven writhing feet of bushmaster.

He'd known it was a bushmaster. Anything else would have been too forgiving, too easy, less deadly. With a bushmaster, it wasn't so much the strength of the venom that killed as it was the sheer quantity of poison the snake could pump into an animal, any kind of animal, including a man.

Moonlight moved with the snake's body, sliding across black-and-gray scales smudged in brownish orange. The wet grass made no sound, not a rustle or a snap as the creature twisted and turned upon itself, its nightly prowl interrupted, its dinner—compliments of Jackson—frozen in fear in the flimsy stick-and-string box trap not a yard away.

Jackson had taken out four of the guards and come away with only a bruised rib cage from a reverse punch he hadn't seen coming, and a knife wound from a blade he most definitely had not seen coming. The cut was a diagonal slash across his chest, but he'd reacted quickly enough to keep the blade from going deep.

He didn't think his odds were anywhere near as good with the bushmaster. The animal was riled, and Jackson's own energy levels were high enough to be sending out all kinds of attack signals. They were in a standoff for the moment, but he doubted that it was going to last.

He readied himself to make a jump in any direction away from the deadly fangs. His muscles twitched in anticipation. His concentration focused on the snake with an intensity that blocked out the rest of the world.

When the snake made its move, he'd have maybe a second to make a countermove. He wasn't ready to die, and if the snake got him, he'd be dead and Sugar would end up in the clutches of evil personified.

Anger filtered into his concentration, but on the next breath he let it go. Anger would only slow him down when the time came to—

Move! Instinct propelled him into a vertical jump. The snake struck, and somebody let out a bloodcurdling scream, but it wasn't him. He'd been so focused on the snake, he'd been oblivious to the other threats in the forest. He didn't wait around to see who had taken the deadly strike. The voice hadn't been female, so he ran like hell, sending up prayers of gratitude for all reptiles.

The crazed screaming and pleading riveted everyone's gaze up toward the shadow-filled forest. Sugar felt Jen tense behind her, felt a ripple of awareness flow through the three guards. They knew it was one of their own.

A burst of gunfire split the night and fear surged through her body. Jackson was up there. She slashed at the ropes binding her and Jen together.

Sher Chang came crashing out of the kitchen cottage, shouting orders, and two of the remaining guards charged up the hill, guns at the ready.

A sob broke from her throat. She didn't want it to end like this, with death and destruction overwhelming all the life she'd nurtured on Cocorico, including Jackson's.

Especially Jackson's.

She struggled with the tiny blade, cutting herself more than once, trying desperately to get free before Sher Chang took notice of them again.

Her efforts were in vain.

The giant lumbered toward them at surprising speed, stopping just short of his prisoners. His eyes grew wide as he looked past her, out over the ocean. Sugar shifted her attention from him to the beach, and found it already gone. The fog was rolling in, consuming everything in its path, obscuring everything in its wake.

A controlled and powerful yell, "*Aaaiiieeeyah*," jerked her head around. She saw Jackson coming out of the night like an apparition—flying through the air in a high leap, one leg stretched out in front of him, the other tucked in close to his body—and connecting with the underside of Sher Chang's chin. The brute's head snapped backward, and he stumbled, but he didn't go down.

"Jackson!" she yelled, warning him of the two men rushing at him from behind.

With the grace of poetry in motion, he pivoted on his foot and sidekicked the first man in the midsection. Jen tripped the second.

"*Huh-yeeah!*" Jackson punched and ducked, avoiding a kick, then came up inside the kicking range and hooked his opponent around the neck, taking him down with a knee smash to the groin.

The second man took a kick to the collarbone, and Sugar swore she heard something break. She'd never seen such controlled violence, such unleashed power. Jackson looked bigger than life, his muscles pumped up, his veins tracking ridges across his arms and chest. He yelled again, coming back into a fighting stance, the sound full of controlled force.

Sher Chang was waiting for him, a murderous glint in his eye. The fog thickened around the two fighters. Sugar cut the last of her and Jen's ropes and rolled to her feet. The old man took up a fighting stance next to Jackson.

He would be crushed, Sugar thought. Between Sher Chang's humongous bulk and Jackson's lightning fast-power, Jen didn't have a prayer of doing anything except getting in the way and getting himself hurt.

She was wrong. The last thing she saw was Jen launching himself at the giant and Jackson following. The fog took them from her view, leaving only sound. All too quickly the fight was over and silence reigned.

Not a breath disturbed the air. She held herself in place, tensed and wary, not daring to move for fear of what she might find—or of what might find her.

TWELVE

"Sugar?" Jackson's voice rang out, sounding distant and vague.

Relief flooded her veins and buckled her knees, dropping her to the ground. She'd expected the worst: Sher Chang looming up out of the fog with his huge awful hands grabbing for her. "I'm here, over here."

Jackson was beside her in seconds, kneeling next to her, a warm presence in the earthbound cloud that had become their world.

"Are you okay? Did they hurt you?" he asked, his mouth close to her ear, his arms strong and sure around her.

"No. I'm not hurt," she said. "Sher Chang wanted to save the pain for later. How's Jen?"

He called out in Chinese and the old man answered.

"He's tying the bastard," he told her. "We don't have much time, Sugar. We have to leave."

"Leave?" Her brow wrinkled in confusion. Why did they have to leave? They'd won, hadn't they?

"There're nine men in a *jiu*, and I only got six," he said, answering the unspoken question in her voice. "The snake got one, and Jen got Chang. That leaves one loose *budoka* with a gun."

A feeling of dread skittered through her, momentarily sidetracking her other concern. "The man, the one who was screaming, was he bitten?"

"It was a bushmaster," Jackson said, without sounding pleased that he'd been right. "I don't think he has much—" The whirring grind of the plane engine starting interrupted him. He swore viciously, coming to his feet. He shouted something in Chinese and pushed her to the ground. "Stay down!"

He slipped away in the fog, and thirty seconds later a burst of gunfire streaked through the white night from her distant right, blasting away toward the beach and the plane.

If Jackson hit anything it would be a miracle, she thought, and if he didn't, it would be a disaster. No matter how good the pilot was, he couldn't get out of the bay without damaging the plane and probably himself, not with zero visibility. Baolian's force had arrived at high tide, and the tide had been going out ever since. By now there would be a barrier of rocks sticking up like jagged teeth across the mouth of the small cove, impossible to maneuver through. If the pilot tried to take off from inside the bay, the fog gave him less than a fifty-fifty chance of not flying into the cliffs wrapping around her home. He was sure to crash.

Another burst of gunfire tore through the air. On the other hand, if Jackson hit the plane's gas tank, all of her worrying about the fog and rocks and crashing was moot.

The engine wound up tighter and tighter, and Jackson reappeared at her side.

"Ran out of ammo," he said, disgusted, putting his hand on the small of her back more to locate her than as a sign of affection. Over his shoulder, he spoke in Chinese, and Jen took up the fight using Sher Chang's automatic weapon.

Jackson swore. "We'll never do it."

"What?" she asked.

"Hit the friggin' gas tank when you can't even see your hand in front of your face."

"You were *trying* to hit the gas tank?"

"Blow that sucker right out of the water." He cursed again. "I hope to hell he can't see any better than we can. Maybe he'll hit a cliff or something, one of the jetties."

Sugar was horrified. Trying to stop the man was understandable, wishing his death was beyond her comprehension.

"You can't mean that," she said, moving away from him in shock.

She didn't get very far before he pulled her back to his side. His face came down real close to hers.

"I mean it, Sugar, every damn word. You've been living in a paradise where all creatures are created equal and they're all sweet and kind." He tightened his hold on her. "I'll be the first to admit that not killing the snake turned out great for us, but the real world just gate-crashed the rest of your party. If the pilot gets away, we lose whatever advantage we might have at this point. This isn't a game to these people. They're out for blood, yours and mine, and I'm not going to let them have it."

Sugar tried not to cringe under the force of his words, or scoot away from him out of fear. This was the side of him she'd only glimpsed, the warrior side. His muscles were tense, his body on the edge of superhuman alertness, still ready to strike. He smelled of sweat and man, of danger . . . and of flowers. The scent was faint but familiar, from one of her wild orchid species.

She was bewildered. How could a man laugh, tease, and pick flowers one moment, then fight with the blood lust of survival rushing through his veins the next?

"Dammit, Sugar, you're trembling. Why?" he asked, rolling her over so they were lying face-to-face.

Her gaze lowered, and she stared mutely at the dragon, at a loss for words. Though they were less than a handbreadth away, wisps of fog floated between them, making the creature appear and reappear as if it were flying through clouds. She couldn't tell Jackson he frightened her. He'd just saved her life, using the very skills and convictions she found frightening.

"Are you sure you're not hurt?" he asked.

"No. It's just—" She never got the chance to tell him. An explosion rent the air, sending a concussion of sound and energy rolling through Cocorico.

Jackson pulled her into his arms, holding her tightly while a fireworks panorama of the plane's destruction upon the cliffs backlit the night. Streamers of red and yellow arced into the sea, too bright to be subdued by the fog.

She expected him to let out a victory whoop, but he was silent. When the last of the visible debris and fire fell from the sky, he rested his forehead on hers and whispered in Chinese, the words solemn, like a benediction for the dead.

Pain lanced her breast. Death was raining on her garden, a place where life had ruled, and she was helpless to stop it.

They slowly rose to their feet, helping each other, and she felt him bow in the direction of the accident, a short but definite lowering of his head in deference to the killed pilot.

No, she definitely did not understand him, a man who played naked in ocean pools, who kissed her as if life began and the sun rose when their lips touched, a man who worked side by side with her in the gardens of Cocorico; and then became a force of destruction, wishing death on an enemy he honored when his wish was fulfilled.

"How long will the fog hold?" He brushed his thumb across her cheek in a gesture of tenderness that confused her even more.

She'd been wrong.

"All night," she said. "Unless the wind comes up."

"Then let's pray for wind." He bent his head to place a kiss upon her brow. She closed her eyes, squeezing them tight against the tears threatening to fall. Two men had died that night, others had been harmed, and she'd been exposed. Nothing was ever going to be the same.

Jen spoke then, a rattling stream of words, much closer to them than she'd thought.

"We have to go," Jackson said. "The men I took out will be coming around any minute, and I only had time to tie three of them."

"What . . . what are you going to do with them?" She couldn't allow more deaths. Murder would put him forever out of her reach.

"There isn't much more I can do," he said. "They're already disarmed. The important thing is that we're not here if there are any reinforcements arriving."

Her gratitude was a palpable sensation, causing her to sigh in relief. As awful as the night had been so far, it wasn't going to get any worse. Now all she had to do was reasonably and calmly explain her position on leaving the island. The time had come to let him go. She'd rather be left with her sadness than for their last moments together to end in an argument.

"I can't leave Cocorico, Jackson." And she couldn't. She didn't need to make a decision, only face the facts. Her whole life was on the island. She wouldn't abandon everything she'd sacrificed for, everything she'd built. This was her sanctuary, the place where she was safe; she felt it emotionally even with all the physical evidence to the contrary. She couldn't leave it to go with a stranger, for that's what Jackson was, what he'd always been. She'd only been fooling herself to think differently.

"Yes, you can," he said.

"No," she said patiently. "I've got my work and the—"

"What you've got," he interrupted, his voice harsh, his hold on her tightening, "is eight men and no place to put them. They win by default. We can have them picked up, maybe even make some money off them, but unless you feel like running a damned prisoner-of-war camp, we'll be safer off the island."

"Money?" she repeated, uncertain of what he meant and a little leery of his anger. She hadn't wanted to fight, but neither would she be bullied.

"Yes, money. I'm a bounty hunter, remember? And we've got over half a ton of Baolian's finest. I can think of two shippers right off the top of my head who will pay to have this scum behind bars."

A light breeze swirled through the fog, dispersing the water droplets and lightly lifting the veil of haze.

"They'll destroy my home," she said in defense of her reasoning. Men who had come to kill would think nothing of ransacking the bungalow and the cottage. Her one consolation was hoping a smart one among them might know better than to tear apart the garden, their only source of food.

"What they'll destroy is you, Sugar." He grasped her hand, reinforcing his words. "If I can get someone here by first light, the buildings will be fine. But we have to leave now. Come on. Show me the way."

She pulled herself free and stepped back, frustrated at his inability to understand. "Listen to me, Jackson." Her voice rose despite her effort to remain calm. "I don't have anyplace else to go, no place left to run. This is it for me, the last hiding place."

"There's no such thing as a hiding place, and there's no damn future in running from anything. You've got me now." He reached for her again, but she moved back.

The wind stirred more vigorously, revealing the hard set of his jaw. Sweat made his skin glisten. Moonlight carved planes and shadows in his face and down the muscles in his arms. She wanted to touch him, to soothe away the implacable frown tightening his mouth, but she held back.

"I'll show you how to leave, or Jen can—he's always known about the pirate's door—but I'm staying. I can hide up in the hills. They'll never find me, and when they're gone, I'll come back."

"No." Jackson shook his head, adamant. She wasn't making any sense. Whatever security she'd had in her tropical paradise had disappeared the minute Sher Chang landed. Baolian would know where her henchman had gone and why, and when he didn't come back with her prizes, she would send another.

Sugar had to know those facts as well as he; she was the one who'd spent three years of her life hiding from the Dragon Queen of the South China Sea. Logic obviously wasn't driving her or she'd be the one dragging him out of there. That left her emotions as the culprit, and it wasn't too difficult to follow those to a conclusion. She was more afraid of facing the outside world than she was of facing Baolian.

He released a long-drawn-out breath. He should

have made love to her before now to deepen the bond between them, then they wouldn't be having this ridiculous conversation. He didn't want to resort to carting her off bodily, but he wasn't above cave man tactics.

"You're coming with me, Sugar."

"I'll only be a danger to you," she said, her argument taking on the undertones of a plea. "Once I leave Cocorico, I'm the kiss of death to anyone I'm with."

Jackson stared at her for all of five seconds before he burst out laughing. He couldn't help it.

The fog lifted more while he continued to laugh, enough for him to watch her confusion turn into irritation and then downright anger.

"There's nothing funny about it."

He begged to differ and bent down to her eye level to give her a succinct explanation. His grin was a mile wide.

"Someday, Sugar, for my pleasure and your sexual edification, I will teach you the 'kiss of death.' Until then, rest assured that it's a special favor to be bought off a Bangkok hooker and not you."

Even in the moonlight, he could see her blush. "You're insufferable."

"Probably, but I'm also right. You're coming with me, no matter how scared you are to leave your little hideaway."

"I am not scared. I'm being practical."

He bit back a curse. He'd had no idea she had such a stubborn streak. Words weren't getting him anywhere. Action was his only recourse. "I think you're making a mistake, but I don't have time to change your mind. Get a few things together, whatever you'll need up in the hills. I'll rest easier knowing you won't have to come back here after I'm gone."

She acquiesced after a moment's hesitation, giving him a short nod before heading toward the bungalow.

He followed a few paces behind. He had never considered himself a very good liar, at least around his brother. With Cooper, it had always seemed that the more vital it was to weave a good story, the less likely he had been to come up with one. He had never successfully lied his way out of a major piece of trouble.

Sugar obviously didn't have Cooper's years of experience to guide her. She'd bought his story, and he'd been lying through his teeth. She would be off the island before he was.

Inside her bedroom, Sugar went first to the closet and removed the box containing Jackson's things. She knew she had to keep moving or her heart would break.

He was leaving.

"You're going to need this stuff once you're off the island," she said, carrying the box over to her bed, willing the tremors out of her voice.

He was leaving. She'd expected to have more notice, time for a good-bye and an apology, time to prepare herself for loneliness.

"I'll give you the charts of the local waters," she went on. "You can pick your island, but I recommend St. Vincent. It's the closest." She opened the box and stepped back, giving him access to the contents.

The first thing he picked up was the gun. He checked the clip, then tucked the weapon into the waistband of his pants. The wallet came next. He opened it up and thumbed through the bills.

"It's all there," she said, giving in to a nominal degree of anger—which was so much better than giving in to heartbreak.

"I wouldn't know if it weren't. I'm just checking my resources." He continued looking through the pockets, checking credit cards and his identification.

"You don't know how much money you carry around in your wallet?" She knew, and it was a lot. He should be more aware of his cash, of his situation . . . of what he was leaving behind.

"I usually have a general idea, but it's been kind of a wild few months." He glanced up, an indecipherable expression on his face. "Did you find anything else in my wallet interesting?"

"I wasn't interested in your money," she said defensively, trying in vain to hold on to her anger. "I was only looking for a phone number or an address or something so I could have Cooper contacted."

"I never did find your radio." He refolded the wallet and slipped it into the pocket of the drawstring pants. "You did use a radio, didn't you?"

"Yes. It's in the pantry, under the floorboards." It didn't matter what he knew now. Nothing mattered.

He lifted his head a fraction, as if to say, Ah yes, of course, the perfect place—but no smile graced his mouth and only a hint of impatience warmed the depths of his eyes. He was the warrior, looking through her to the next move.

"Get your clothes together, Sugar," he told her, glancing away to pick up the rest of his things and put them in his pockets. "I have to go."

That was right. He was in a hurry. She'd forgotten for a moment. There was no more time left for words of the love he'd thought he felt, not when his freedom beckoned like a fire in the night.

Moving around the room, she stuffed clothes and a few personal items into a canvas bag. The wind was picking up, gaining strength and setting the jalousies quivering. She wished she'd thought ahead to have a present for him, something for him to remember her by besides a few ragged pieces of clothing.

Her hand lingered on a conch shell, then passed it by to pick up her comb to put in the bag. Every souvenir shop in the West Indies sold conch shells. The only unique thing she had on Cocorico were the endangered flora species, and she couldn't quite see him bothering to take a plant home, or her being dumb enough to give him one.

She grabbed extra socks for her bag. Most of what she needed she could get off the land, including food, water, and shelter. She wouldn't starve up-country, but she wanted to take cooking utensils and a few food items out of the cottage. She wanted to take him. He hadn't seen that part of the island, where the mists gathered in the trees, where it rained in the sunshine. The trade winds always blew up-country, cooling down the heat and wafting soft against a person's skin. The mountain trails were precarious, the wildlife abundant. The land was rugged, open, and free, the vistas went on forever and ever. It was a good place for a dragon's lair.

Jack Sun preferred San Francisco.

He could believe whatever he wanted, but she knew Shulan was telling the truth about his heritage. They both carried Sun Yi's blood—and for that, Baolian wanted him dead.

She stopped with a sweatshirt clutched in her fist, turning to look at him over her shoulder.

"You'll be careful, won't you?" Her voice was softer than she'd meant it to be, the warning more personal, revealing a level of emotion she would be wise to hide.

She needn't have worried he'd read too much into her words. He only gave her a wry glance and said, "I'm not the one you need to be worrying about."

"I'll be fine." Her chin lifted. One way or the other, she would survive being alone again. The days would melt into one another like sand into the sea, and before long his face would fade from her memory along with the sound of his voice.

But not his kiss. What she'd felt with his kiss would never fade.

"I'm sure you will be," he said, showing more confidence in her than she would have expected.

Maybe too much confidence. If she wasn't supposed to worry about him or herself, then who? No one was in more trouble, unless—

"Shulan never meant you harm," she said, interceding for her friend. Whatever revenge he might exact should not include the young Asian woman. "She was only trying to save someone she cared about."

He let out a hard laugh. "She didn't even know me until she dragged me off the beach."

"No, but she knew about you. She knew she had a brother, and as far as Cooper would go to avenge you, she went to protect you. No more, no—"

The wooden shutters on the window snapped open with a crash, bouncing against the wall, then flapping back to hang crookedly. Wind swirled through the room, rattling bottles and displacing papers.

"Let's get the hell out of here," he growled, reaching for her canvas bag and leading the way out of the bungalow.

They met Jen on the windswept verandah, and the news he delivered made Jackson swear.

"What's wrong?" she asked.

"Sher Chang is missing." He grabbed her by the arm and propelled her down the steps, following Jen. "Whatever else you thought you needed, you're going to have to do without."

"I thought he was tied," she said, running to keep up with him.

"He was, but it's damn hard to tie a snake and make it hold." The mists had lifted enough for the moon to light their way, but wisps of fog still swirled across the ground, driven by the wind.

"What do you mean?" she asked.

"Sher Chang, his name translates to 'Chang the Snake.' Jen calls him Manushi, after an Asiatic pit viper that's fine as long as it's picking on something smaller than itself, but pretty damn ineffectual on anything bigger."

Another snake, she thought in dismay. Suddenly her island was crawling with them, and they had brought discord and destruction to her gardens. The bushmaster and she could have lived in wary harmony, but ineffectual or not, she didn't want to deal with a human snake, especially alone.

"What are the chances of you being able to get someone here tomorrow to pick these men up?"

"Good, but better for the day after. I have some connections in Brazil I can count on for help."

The increasing wind made further discussion difficult. She would wait until they were inside the icehouse. They were nearly there.

To their right, the forest fluttered and swayed in the wind, all the leaves rustling together and sounding like a larger version of the four-tiered waterfall. The clearing where she'd thought he'd been sleeping was directly ahead. Palms flanked both sides of the grassy area. A frond tore free as they entered the clearing and blew against her, making her stumble.

Jackson lost his grip on her and she went down, catching herself with her hands. The wind wasn't knocked out of her, but she gasped anyway—first in outrage, then out of fear.

Directly in front of her face, less than two feet away, was a box trap holding a jungle runner. There was only one person who would have dared to trap one of her animals—Jackson Daniels, the man who dared anything and defied the rest. She would have given him both

barrels of her anger if she hadn't been frozen in place by
the hypnotic stillness of the bushmaster less than a foot
farther away, stalking its corralled dinner.

Its tongue flickered in the moonlight, feeling her
heat and chilling her to the bone.

"Don't move," Jackson whispered.

The warning was unnecessary. Her muscles were
numb; not so the snake's. Its head silently slid forward,
searching, and a bolt of adrenaline shot through her,
searing a path to every nerve ending she possessed.

She sensed more than saw Jackson drawing his gun.

"No," she breathed, and the bushmaster coiled in
upon itself, reacting to her voice.

Moonbeams played along the whole awesome
length of the reptilian beast, shining off the slick-
skinned body and revealing where its tail crossed the
forest path and made sinuous tracings in the mix of soil
and sand. The bushmaster was huge and powerful, an
animal to be reckoned with on its own terms.

Jackson moved again, and once again she warned
him off.

"No." She kept her voice calm and low, soothing.
The snake was looking directly at her, holding her gaze
with its snake's eyes. The forked tongue flickered at her
again. She didn't respond with another bolt of fear, but
with acceptance. She was well within striking distance
of one of the most formidable creatures on the face of
the earth. It would either bite her or not, and for reasons she didn't fully understand, her money was on not.

All around them the storm built in strength and intensity, but the creatures in the glade held their places

in the deadly tableau of woman, beast, and man. Jen, far in the lead, had gone on ahead, unaware of the danger behind him.

The snake glided forward, head held high, stretching its length out. It seemed endless, longer than herself by twice as much. Below the sound of the wind, she heard the soft, hissing slither of scales sliding across the grass. Lord, she prayed she was right about the thing not biting her.

Jackson had never felt so useless. A venom factory was closing in on the woman he loved, and he didn't dare take a chance and shoot it. He wouldn't put it past her to throw herself in front of a speeding bullet to save a damn snake. She wouldn't make it, of course, she wasn't that fast. But the damn snake was fast—fast enough to get her before he could pull the trigger.

He was standing so still his body hurt. Only seconds had passed since she'd fallen, and only seconds more would pass before the confrontation was over, one way or the other.

The bushmaster kept gliding across the grass, moving closer and closer to where she knelt at Jackson's feet. The trapped lizard was paralyzed with fear.

With a rapid action Jackson never could have beaten, the snake struck and sank its fangs into its prey. Jackson's stomach and heart both plummeted, taking ten years off his life, even though it was the jungle runner the bushmaster had chosen, box trap and all, and not Sugar.

The lizard struggled, but the bushmaster held firm, pulling its body in close to give it more strength and leverage. The box trap disintegrated under the thrashing it took. Jackson wasn't waiting around for the final scene. He reached down for Sugar, ready to pull her to her feet and get the hell out of there—but once again the snake was faster. When Jackson grabbed Sugar, the snake grabbed him, its tail coiling up from underneath her arm and wrapping around his wrist, binding them together with a powerful squeeze of its body.

Sweet Lord, he prayed, instantly hyperventilating, his eyes glazing over with shock. The snake was curled around him like a bracelet, tying him to Sugar, while it fought the lizard to the death.

No one would believe it.

He didn't believe it.

The bushmaster's body was cool and dry, all sinuous, moving muscle wrapping around his arm. Black-and-gray markings ran together as the snake slid and coiled around him, showing flashes of its orange underbelly. The thought of shooting it crossed his mind once, like a streak of lightning, and was just as quickly discarded. The snake had spared him twice.

The lizard jerked in its last throes of death, and the bushmaster slowly uncoiled, releasing him and Sugar. Neither of them so much as twitched until the snake was nothing more than a shadow moving in the forest.

Maybe he'd dreamed the whole surreal incident.

A shudder rippled through his body. He hadn't dreamed anything. He and Sugar had just tangled with a bushmaster, been caressed by the reptile. By rights, they should both be suffering their own death throes.

"Jackson?" Her voice was soft, barely a whisper.

"Yeah?"

"I think we should get out of here."

"Yeah."

He crouched down and helped her to her feet. She was as unsteady as he was, her knees jelly, her breath coming as rapidly as his. He'd been mistaken when he'd thought she wasn't reacting with the same spine-tingling distress he'd felt.

"It wasn't going to hurt us, you know," she said, not sounding overly convinced.

He let out a deep breath. "No, I didn't know that. Are you okay?"

"Fine." Her voice was shaking too much for him to believe her. "How about you?"

"Doing great. Just great." He didn't sound any better than she did.

Jen yelled at them from the icehouse, exhorting them to hurry. Jackson tightened his hold on her, and together they made their way up to the old building at the base of the cliff. Jen beckoned them inside.

Jackson looked down at her. "I thought you said he knew the way out of here."

"That's it." She stepped inside and gestured at the wood planks covering the southern wall. They were old and scarred and thick, like ship's siding. He remembered them from when he'd had tea with Jen.

"Cocorico was a pirate's cove long before it became mine," she continued. "The better living is on this side of the island, but the better mooring is on the other side. So the brigands blasted a tunnel. They built the door to keep unwanted visitors out."

"And you've been using it to keep me in," he said, disgusted with himself. He should have seen it before, what with Jen camped out in front of the damn icehouse night and day. His consolation was in knowing that if he had escaped, he wouldn't have been there to save her from Sher Chang.

Jen hurried to the back of the shack, and Jackson heard the sound of a heavy chain running through metal rings. Chances were, even if he'd realized where the door was, he wouldn't have been able to open it.

The wooden planks moved, swinging inward and taking up most of the remaining space. Sugar squeezed through the opening left between the outer wall and the door. He followed her into a narrow portal. Jen was ahead of them, lighting their way with a flashlight and ordering them to keep up.

The tunnel was cool and damp, unhappily reminding him of the river that ran above their heads. The passageway curved through the rock, making it impossible to see too far ahead or too far behind. Jen's flashlight beam bounced off jagged walls and an uneven floor.

Without warning, they turned a corner and stumbled out onto a beach. It was as if the tunnel walls had suddenly disappeared to be replaced with sea and sand, trees and the night sky. The wind that had buffeted them in the glade didn't exist on this side of the island. The storm had been confined to her home and gardens, a meteorological anomaly he wasn't going to begin to try to understand.

He breathed his first easy breath in hours. There

was a whaleboat in the bay with a big outboard motor hanging off the stern. He hadn't known what to expect, but a dugout canoe wouldn't have surprised him.

Sugar felt her heart constrict at the sight of the boat. Wild roses twined their way across the bow and down either side, along with paintings of oleander, hibiscus, frangipani, the yellow blossoms of nightsage, all manner of orchids, and the strikingly tropical lobster-claw helconia with its spikelike orange flowers set against the turquoise blue of the hull. Henry kept the boat in good repair. She used it to get to parts of the island that were inaccessible by an overland route. She had never used it to leave or even to go beyond Shark Alley. There was no place she could go without putting someone in danger. There was no place she could go now. She could only stand on the beach and watch Jackson leave.

He and Jen were walking toward the dock, speaking in Chinese to each other. She knew she had to go down and show them where she kept her charts and compass. A course of north by northeast would get them to St. Vincent in little over an hour. From there, the world was at his feet.

Briefly, she allowed herself to wonder if he would ever come back. Then she squelched the thought as hopeless and forced herself to move. She got no farther than a yard before she was captured from behind.

A strangled scream lodged in her throat, cut off by the huge sweaty hand clamped over her mouth. What little sound she made was drowned by the pounding surf. Neither Jackson nor Jen looked back.

She kicked at her attacker, squirming within the

ironlike bands of his arms. He was hauling her back to the tunnel, and what she knew was a fate worse than death. All of her years of planning and caution were coming to naught. She'd always thought it would be easy to die, that she would be in control of the moment, able to choose death over torture. But she wasn't going to have a choice. The beast holding her, Chang the Snake, had promised rape and mutilation, and death only when it was granted by Fang Baolian.

Helpless rage boiled up within her. The Dragon Whore would not reduce her to less than a woman. With all her strength, she tightened the muscles in her arms and smashed her elbow back into Sher Chang's torso, catching him just under the rib cage.

He let her go with an *ummph*, and she screamed bloody murder.

Jackson whirled around and took off up the beach at a dead run. Sher Chang had found them. He and Sugar were on the ground, and he had her by the ankle. The brute crawled and lunged through the sand after her, trying for a better hold. She rolled over to fight him off, and Jackson winced. Damn bad move, Sugar, he thought, unless you can get in a good kick before he crushes you.

She did, right to the bastard's groin. Howling, the giant recoiled, cupping his injured manhood, his face a mask of rage and pain. Jackson didn't give him a chance to recover. There was no such thing as a fair fight when lives were on the line. He caught Sher Chang on the side of the head with the heel of his foot, and the giant crumpled to the sand in sudden and absolute silence.

Once again, the two of them were left in the moonlight, breathing too fast with their hearts pounding. If another snake came out of the night and so much as looked cross-eyed at her, Jackson was shooting first and asking questions later. He'd had enough.

He helped her to her feet and steadied her while they caught their breaths. Behind him, Jen started up the big outboard. He saw her look over his shoulder, saw dismay cloud her face. He understood her reaction; she thought she was staying on the island alone, the way she'd been for so long.

He wasn't about to tell her any different. She'd know soon enough.

She shifted her gaze to meet his, and the sadness in her eyes tore at him. He'd never seen such a bleak surrender to the inevitable.

"It's time," she said so softly he almost didn't hear the words.

He tightened his hold on her arms, trying to give her his strength. She'd had a rebel's spirit once. She still did when it came to fighting him, but she needed to find enough of it again to fight her real enemy, Fang Baolian.

"Jackson, before you leave . . ." Her gaze slid away from his. "I—I want you to know that if I could have chosen a man to come, if I could have chosen a man to love, I would have chosen you. . . ." Her voice trailed off in a whisper full of regrets.

A single tear slipped free, and he captured it with his finger. She was so beautiful, so strong. He wanted to kiss her, before she got so mad at him he'd be lucky to get within ten feet of her, but there was no help for it. They were out of time.

"I want you to remember that, Sugar, no matter what," he said, just before he bent down, picked her up, and hauled her over his shoulder. Jen had the boat idling, waiting for them.

THIRTEEN

Jackson stood on the balcony of his hotel room. Below him was an enclosed garden, a small jungle sweet with the scent of flowers. Above him was a dark sky preparing to give way to dawn. To his left was Sugar, stonily silent, staring down at the inky profusion of plants.

She hadn't spoken to him since he and Jen had dragged her off the Kingstown docks and as far away from the ocean as they could get on foot. He'd offered to take her to her father's house, but she'd acted like he'd offered to help her murder baby harp seals. The last place she would go, she'd told him with anger sparking her eyes, was anywhere near anyone she cared about. So she'd gone with him. He hadn't missed the not-so-subtle insult in her decision.

Jen had the room on the other side of Sugar's, but he'd gone to bed after making a phone call to Shulan.

Jackson had made his own phone call. Cooper would be on St. Vincent by nightfall and have a crew on

Cocorico before that. Jackson was to stay out of it. Cooper would rather lose the bounty than take a chance on losing him again. He hadn't had to say it twice. Jackson was bone-tired. Even under Sugar's benign house arrest, his nerves had been taut, his body harboring unconscious tension. With freedom had come release and exhaustion. He was ready to collapse.

The problem was, the place he wanted to collapse was in Sugar's bed, preferably with her next to him. He would feel safer that way, and she would be safer. He had not been invited, though, and from the look on her face, it would be a cold day in hell before she so much as spoke to him again, let alone asked him into her bed. He had kidnapped her, an act that had evened up the felonies in their relationship, but was unlikely to get him anything more intimate.

He sighed and looked back out into the night. Cooper had cried on the phone. That had shaken him up. The last time he'd heard Cooper cry was when their mom had died. Nobody had shed a tear for Old Man Daniels, not even his only son, but Cooper had cried for Jackson.

A knock sounded on the door, and he pushed himself away from the balcony railing. His credit cards had been canceled due to his untimely demise, but he'd had enough cash in American dollars to grease a few wheels of comfort, like having breakfast served at four-thirty in the morning.

The inn's proprietress, a groggy but congenial black woman, had done the cooking herself, explaining that her chef didn't come to work for another hour. She rolled in a cart laden with coffee, freshly baked muffins, two covered omelettes, a double order of bacon for Jackson, and a basket of fruit. He helped her push it out on the balcony and set a few of the items, along with a vase of flowers, onto a small table.

After the proprietress left, he walked over and lightly touched Sugar's shoulder.

"I wish you would eat something. We've had a long night."

Her answer was the same one he'd been getting since he'd carried her aboard the boat. "You have to take me back."

"You don't have to live in exile." The words had become his standard answer. "I'm not going to spend the rest of my life in hiding, and Baolian wants me as badly as she wants you."

"Not quite," she said, sounding as tired as he felt.

He conceded the point with silence. He was merely a possible threat to Baolian's empire and had only hurt her ego. Sugar had actually cut the royal tush.

"Cocorico isn't safe anymore anyway, Sugar. It's on the map now. Every pirate and bounty hunter from here to Singapore has just put a big *X* on their Caribbean charts for 'marks the spot.'"

"I know." She wrapped one arm around her waist and buried her face in her other hand. Her anger was giving way to desolation, a transition he would rather not have witnessed, yet he knew it was all part of the process of letting go. She'd lost so much in the last twelve hours: her sense of security—however false it might have been—her home, her work, her means of support, yet her insistence on returning hinted at something more. Cocorico was no longer safe, even she admitted it, but a part of her still saw the place as a sanctuary.

From what, though?

He moved closer and slipped his arm around her shoulders, enfolding her to his side. After a moment's hesitation, she sank against him.

This was where she belonged, he thought, tightening his hold. For reasons he didn't fully understand, he needed her next to him, always. He needed her in his life. She had become a part of him, or he a part of her. He didn't know which or if it even made a difference. There had been only a few women in his life and he'd loved each of them, but Sugar entranced him beyond romantic love. She was an endless mystery to be explored, a primeval Eve, virginal and ripe, fecund. Where she worked, life blossomed, what she nurtured thrived. Leaving her alone in her gardens had been impossible from the moment he'd seen her. Even if Sher Chang had never shown up, he would not have left without her. He would have cajoled, enticed, seduced, whatever it took to keep her by his side.

Frustration tightened his jaw. She was by his side now, but he was no closer to keeping her than he'd ever been.

"You can't go back, not until things change," he said, wondering who he was lying to the most, her or himself. "Baolian has to be dealt with, one way or the other."

"I don't have anyplace else to go, Jackson." She

shook her head, and her soft curls caught and held the differing angles of moonlight. "Noplace else."

"We'll figure out a plan. Come on." He led her over to the table. "Things will look better if you have something to eat and get some rest."

He already had a plan, a half dozen of them, but the decisions were hers to make. All he could do was console, cajole, entice, and do his damnedest to seduce.

He pulled out her chair and poured her a cup of coffee. When she was settled, he sat down on the opposite side of the table and reached for a muffin.

"You'll have some money coming from the bounty," he said, "enough to keep you going for a few months, give you some time to figure out what you want."

"I don't want bounty money."

She might as well have said she didn't want blood money. He stopped with the muffin halfway to his plate. His eyes narrowed. "Don't judge me."

Sugar inwardly flinched at the coldness in his voice. Nothing was the same since they'd left Cocorico. Whatever closeness they'd achieved had been artificially induced by captivity, nothing else. She felt more alone with him now than she'd ever felt on her island.

"I'm sorry," she said, stumbling around for the right words. "I didn't mean that the way it sounded." And she knew it had sounded very holier-than-thou. "I don't deserve the bounty money. You and Jen saved us."

His gaze dropped to his plate. "You did your part. You'll get your share."

Silence descended with all the awkwardness possible between two people. She poked at her food and sneaked glances at him as he attacked his. Everything was wrong. The rhythms she lived by on Cocorico didn't exist off her island. She didn't fit in, couldn't even make conversation without being misunderstood. She felt alien, vulnerable—and so very guilty.

Cocorico had been more than her sanctuary, it had been her penance. And she was still unforgiven in her own heart.

The telephone rang in Jackson's room, and when he got up to answer it, Sugar gave up the fight. There was one place for her to go, one place she had to go.

Jackson knew she was gone the moment he stepped back out onto the balcony. He checked the garden, but saw nothing, so he ran back into his room and checked the street through his front window. He was in time to see a small figure ducking around the corner, blond hair gleaming by the light of a street lamp.

The rational part of him told him to let her go, but his heart wasn't listening.

Sugar climbed the familiar road heading north out of town and into the hills. The island was beginning to stir, making ready to greet the sun on its daily rise out of the eastern ocean.

She turned off the road onto a leeward lane and followed it to a high stone wall covered with patches of green moss. Vines wound their way across the wall, and small flowering plants nestled in the nooks between mortar and stone. Moisture from the night's rain dripped from the trees, making shallow puddles beneath her feet and reflecting the brightening dawn's light through the protective grove.

Nothing had changed. The place smelled so much like home. She knelt by a wrought-iron gate and jiggled free a loose stone. Inside the exposed cranny, she found the key, her key, hidden low in the wall for a child to reach.

She let herself in and walked around to the ocean side of the house. The house sat up high on a promontory, and the view from the back porch went on forever. On a clear day, a person might even imagine she could see Cocorico on the horizon, floating on the waves of the Caribbean Sea.

It was too early to disturb anyone, so she settled into a big wicker rocking chair under the porch eaves and draped herself with the soft cotton throw folded neatly over its back. The pastel-striped blanket brought back memories of another life full of love and boundless affection, of cuddling up to another warm body to watch the sunset, of being touched and soothed.

Jackson had touched her, deep down inside where the caress would never fade. He'd been a trial and a joy, and he would be missed, never forgotten. But it was best to let him go. She wished they had made love, though. After knowing him, after sharing his kiss, she didn't think she would ever want another man.

He was fine, and strong, and true, and for a while he could have been hers. She should have taken the chance.

As if her thoughts could bring him to her, he appeared at the edge of the porch. She stiffened in the chair, feeling the failure of her escape. He had followed her.

"You shouldn't have come here." She rose to her feet, ready to argue him away. Before she could say anything more, though, another voice entered the moment, one as gentle as the dawn's light, as sweet as the name upon its lips.

"Sugar? Darlin', is that you?"

Sugar turned toward the door, her heart pounding. "Momma."

Jackson's gaze followed Sugar's to a lady dressed in a white linen jumper over a white cotton T-shirt. The style was plain and simplistically lovely. The woman was stunningly beautiful, like an angel, like Sugar. Her hair was the same pale blond, but longer, a riotous tumble of curls pulled into order with a pair of ivory-colored combs. Her eyes were blue, where Sugar's were a silvery gray—and her body was broken, where Sugar's was whole.

The woman leaned heavily on a cane, limping forward to her daughter. She caught the younger woman to her and together they sank into the old rocking chair, crying and holding each other.

Jackson knew that for all practical purposes, he had disappeared off the face of the earth. He also knew he was intruding on a very intimate reconciliation, but he couldn't force himself to back away. The rightness of seeing them together held him where he stood, within hearing distance of all they had to say.

"You're home, Sugar, honey. You're home." The woman's voice broke with emotion. Her hands never stopped clutching at the grown child in her arms. Long blond curls melded with short ones where their heads were bent close together.

"Oh, Momma. I'm sorry."

This was what he'd missed for so many years, missed with an ache that he'd only begun to fill with adulthood —a mother's love. Sugar was being drenched in it, washed clean with the tears they shed.

Innocent people were hurt, crippled, people I love. Her mother had been there the morning Baolian's henchmen had blown up the car, and she'd been crippled by the act of vengeance.

"I've missed you so much," the woman crooned. "You didn't have to stay away because of me. I wrote you a thousan' times, and you still didn't come."

Sugar only shook her head. Jackson understood. If he had brought that kind of destruction down on somebody he loved, he would have exiled himself, too, and there was a good chance it would have taken more than three years for him to get up enough courage to come back.

He watched and waited as the two women held each other and rocked, whispering their words of pain and forgiveness. The sun had completely burned away the night before the creaking of the old chair stopped.

Sugar's mother looked up, directly at him, proving she'd known he was there all along. "Mr. Daniels?"

He nodded, more than a little taken aback by her clear-eyed gaze and the authority in her voice. He now knew where Sugar had gotten her courage.

"My daughter is sleepin'. Will you help me get her in to bed?"

"Yes, ma'am." Not even the thought of a grin crossed his mind, no matter that he'd been trying to get Sugar into bed since the first time they'd met.

"You may call me Arabella."

"Yes, ma'am." He stepped forward and first helped Arabella get to her feet and find her balance with the cane. Then he lifted Sugar into his arms.

Arabella led him into the airy bungalow and to a suite of bedrooms with a connecting bath. Sugar never made a sound as her mother removed her shoes and pulled a light sheet over her. The room was warm without being uncomfortable, with a slight trade-wind breeze ruffling the curtains.

"You mus' be exhausted yourself, Mr. Daniels," Arabella said, giving him a thorough looking over. Her voice was hushed, with just a hint of patois.

"Yes, ma'am, I am. It's been a hel—it's been a long night."

"I would be much obliged if you would 'cept my hospitality. You're welcome to the other room." She said it all with a smile that was both warm and welcoming, impossible to resist even if he had been inclined to resist—which he wasn't.

"Thank you, ma'am."

"Arabella," she insisted.

"Arabella."

"Mr. Daniels—"

"Jackson, please."

"Jackson," she agreed with another smile, then became more serious. "May I be frank?"

The idea made him a little uneasy, but he nodded.

She took a deep breath, as if to steel herself. "I have been unable to help my daughter through her troubles. Travelin' is so painful, and until today, she has refused to come home. She blames herself too much for what happened, 'specially on my account." A small grin teased her mouth. "I'm sure whatever wildness she has she gets from me and not her father."

She looked over at the sleeping Sugar and her face softened. "I love her very much, Jackson, and I'd be much obliged if you would do whatever you can to keep her from goin' back to that island. She deserves a full life, a family, children of her own. I would consider it a blessin' if you could help her"—the small smile returned, at once full of mystery and benevolence, and her blue-eyed gaze lifted to meet his—"in whatever capacity you might be comfortable with."

For pure shock ability, Jackson decided, Arabella Caine took the cake, hands down.

With another gracious smile, she left, moving steadily but awkwardly down the hall. Jackson closed the door after her and crawled into bed with Sugar, pulling her close to keep her safe, and wondering if her mother could have possibly meant everything he'd thought he'd heard in her request.

Jackson didn't know how long he'd been asleep when he heard the door open. Before he could work up his defenses, they were made unnecessary by a woman's voice.

"So, Carolina, is that your dragon boy?"

"I s'pose," another woman answered. "I ain't never seen him with his clothes on."

A moment of knowing silence fell, then was broken by a double fit of bubbling laughter. The door closed, but Jackson could still hear them laughing and talking.

"I jus' knew he was gonna be trouble, him and that ol' Chinee."

"He brought her home, Carolina. I think I can handle his kind of trouble for a long time."

Their voices faded away, but he'd be damned if he wasn't blushing again.

FOURTEEN

When next Jackson woke, late-afternoon sunlight slanted obliquely across the room through the ocean-side window. Sugar was sweetly tousled by his side, still sound asleep, her T-shirt riding up almost to her breasts.

He sighed and gently, so as not to disturb her,

levered himself to a sitting position. Beside the bed was a tray of food: bread, cheese, fruit, vegetables, juice, and what he hoped was a carafe of coffee.

There were two cups, which made sense given Arabella's blessing, but he was still shocked. The other mothers he'd known wouldn't have fed a man they had found in bed with their daughter. In his experience, they were more likely to scream first and ask questions later. Maybe he had fallen into another strange paradise.

His gaze drifted over the tray of food, and he thought longingly of the double order of crisp bacon he'd left uneaten at the inn. None of these women seemed to require meat in their diets, whereas he was to the point of fantasizing about roasting wild boar over an open fire, preferably with a gallon of barbecue sauce handy.

Utterly barbaric. Utterly divine.

He helped himself to a cup of coffee. At least the java, rich and smooth, had a kick to it, and the piece of bread he tasted was more like cake, moist with the flavor of bananas. The cheese was creamy and slightly sweet, and everything was fresher and better than he would have imagined. He chose another piece of bread and was rewarded with the tangy citrus taste of oranges.

Wishing for barbecued pork began to seem misguided when he compared it with the array of delights spread out before him. He picked up a slice of greenish-yellow fruit and bit into it.

A smooth sweetness filled his mouth, instantly reminding him of Sugar's kiss. Warmth flooded his body.

He savored the taste, wondering what it would take to have her, what it would take to keep her. If Sher Chang had not shown up, would she have already been his lover?

He finished the first piece of fruit and took another, enjoying it while he looked the tray over to see what delicacy he would try next. He'd slept so peacefully in her arms. He was rested. All he needed was food—and Sugar. Always Sugar. He'd waited so long, much longer it seemed than he'd even known her.

The tray was beautiful, hand-carved wood inlaid with a design he couldn't quite make out for all the food on top of it. He did recognize the flowers carved and painted on the intricately wrought handles. Their real-life counterparts decorated two of the corners of the tray—large, showy white blooms with reddish centers and a crown of white-and-purple filaments. The fragrant flowers were still attached to their vines, the leaves adding to the beauty of the presentation, the tendrils winding through the fruits and vegetables to tie the whole thing together the way the lianas tied together the forest on Cocorico.

Damn. He'd forgotten about Cocorico. He needed to call the inn and leave a message for Cooper. He picked up another slice of the fruit to take with him to the phone, but before he could move, Sugar stirred.

He looked over his shoulder to find her eyes just opening. She looked dreamy and content curled into the pillows, her hair haloed around her face, soft color blushing her cheeks. Her gaze met his and held, and when she smiled, his heart dropped into the pit of his stomach. All thoughts of Cocorico and Cooper fled in the wake of that shy smile.

"Hi." He turned sideways on the bed, facing her, hoping to hell he didn't sound overly eager for whatever attention she might give him. He was a fool for her, and he liked it far too much to pretend otherwise. For her, he was an open book. Any trace of artifice would have been too much. He was ready, willing, and able to give her the truth in his heart.

"Hi."

"Hungry?" he asked.

She nodded and pushed herself to a sitting position. He reached out to help her, and they ended up very close together as much by accident as by design.

"I'm . . . uh, not sure what this is, but it's good." He took a bite of the fruit as if to say, See how good it is?—before offering her the rest. He felt breathless, waiting for her to take it, and he couldn't remember a time when a woman had left him breathless. Neither could he remember a time when merely looking at a woman's mouth had made him ache.

His fingers lingered on her lips after she ate the fruit from his hand, and he smiled. He'd won something with that small act of acquiescence, but he wasn't sure what.

"It's granadilla," she said, lowering her lashes.

"Granadilla?"

The color heightened in her cheeks. "*Passiflora edulis*. Passion fruit."

"Ah." Maybe that explained the way he felt, as if he had to have her now or forever live without her, that if he let her slip away this time, there would be no other chance.

"Not that kind of passion," Sugar said, daring an upward glance at Jackson. "The passion of the death and resurrection of a god." And surely that was what Jackson was, a man in the image of the God who had made him.

From the safety of her childhood refuge, he looked far less intimidating than he had on Cocorico, but no less beautiful. The tawnyness of his skin was warm and inviting in the late-afternoon sun. His hair was an ebony veil sliding across his chest and draping over her thighs. Looking at him, she felt an indescribable yearning to bury her face in the crook of his neck and cloak herself in the silken strands, to lay her hand over his dragon's heart and feel the life pulse through him on every beat, to somehow take him inside herself and never let him go.

She was in love.

"The god Eros?" he asked, moving closer.

"I'm—I'm not sure. I don't think so." Her heartbeat speeded up with both fear and excitement in response to his nearness. She'd awakened earlier and had found herself lying next to him, his breath blowly softly across the top of her head, his chest a wall of strength at her back. She'd known she should leave, that her presence was a danger to those she loved, but against all odds Jackson made her feel safe. Within the comforting circle of his arms was a haven and a promise, freely given, inviolate, one she was loath to relinquish. So she'd fallen back into a dreamless sleep and awakened once more to find him still by her side.

But this time the dragon was also awake, feeding her from his hand as if she were the wild creature needing to be tamed.

Strange, beautiful man. He was free now, and in some new way so was she. He could leave, find and have any woman to share his life.

"Well, I'm not a god, Sugar, but I do feel resurrected," he said, reaching out to touch her. The calluses on his fingers were rough against her skin, and she reveled in the difference. "Baolian didn't manage to kill me, but she did forfeit my life on that beach, and Shulan took it."

"I know." She looked away, a wave of guilt making it impossible to face him. She had no right to want him the way she did. "I'm sorry for everything, Jackson, for not helping you more."

"Don't be," he said, tilting her chin up. Warm eyes gazed down into hers. "You took my life and held it, and made it into something better than it had been before. You opened up a part of me I didn't know I had, the part that must have been holding on to an image of you for aeons, because that's how long I feel like I've been waiting for you."

"You don't have to say those things."

"Yes, I do, Sugar." The strain of urgency tightened his voice. "In a few hours my life starts up again. As soon as Cooper comes, I go back to being what I am, and I need to know you're going to be a part of me."

He was asking the impossible. She couldn't see

where she would fit into his life. "I don't know what you'll hold on to, Jackson, but you'll always be a part of me." And wasn't that all they could offer each other? Memories of a time that shouldn't have been?

"That's not good enough," he said, sounding damn sure of himself and a little angry. "I want to marry you, Sugar, bind you to me. I want to plant my seed deep inside your womb and watch you blossom with our child."

He'd shocked her. Jackson could tell by the stunned look on her wide-eyed face. He needed to back off. He needed to woo, but he no longer had the patience for words alone. So he kissed her.

A fleeting kiss at first, a mere touching of their mouths. His hands came up to cup her face, and he rested his forehead on hers. "I don't want to spend the rest of my life without you, knowing there was anything more I could have done to win you."

He kissed her again, inhaling her fragrance. He didn't know much about the kind of love he felt for her; it was all too new. But he did know about pleasure, how it tangled around a person's heart and libido, how it imprinted on a body so that the slightest touch from the one who had given it brought the sensations back again. There was a bond in pleasure, intense and intimate.

She wanted him. She'd said as much, said she wanted him until she couldn't see beyond the wanting into love. He was putting his heart on the line, praying he could show her the way.

Her lips were tender beneath his, her breath growing shallow with even their chaste kiss. It emboldened him to do more. In one lithe move, he lowered her to the bed and slid his hand under her shirt, opening his mouth over hers at the same time. She moaned, and a spiral of desire curled through his body down to his groin. Arousal began thrumming through his veins.

Sugar had never known how good a man's weight could feel. He was lying half over her, his palm kneading her breast, one of his thighs fitted in between hers, and she was coming apart from the inside out.

His skin was satiny soft over hard muscle, a sensory delight to her each place they touched. Every move he made, from the seductive grind of his pelvis against hers to the more subtle action of his breath, elicited a response from her physically and emotionally. They were two people moving as one, two halves striving to be a whole, and the path they led each other down was laden with adventure and discovery.

She smoothed her hand over his abdomen and felt the muscles there tighten. The breath soughed from his lips, and he stilled on top of her. When she did nothing else, he angled his mouth closer to her ear and whispered, "Go on, Sugar. Lower."

In answer, her fingers slid downward, over a taut plane of ridged muscles and into a thatch of silky hair. Instinct guided her to encircle him and move her hand up his shaft . . . and back down.

"Ah, Sugar, Sugar." He moved with her, and when her hand came up again, he pushed her T-shirt up and lowered his mouth to her bared breast.

The rhythm they worked together became the vehicle for transcending time and space. The rhythm bridged the distance between their skin, taking them deeper into each other.

Heat and need consumed her, pushed her onward, made her restless with a yearning she felt coursing through her entire body. He laved her other breast, teasing her with his tongue, and still it wasn't enough.

"Jackson." His name came out on a gasp.

He levered himself up to kiss her mouth, then rose to a sitting position, straddling her hips. He stripped his shirt off and reached for hers, all the while watching her with his smoldering green gaze. When he eased off the bed to remove his pants, she lowered her eyes and met those of the dragon. Insatiable beast, he looked as eager to devour her as his master, but the beast was no more eager than she.

How a woman could be half-naked, her mouth swollen from kisses and her breasts blushed from the same, and still look innocent was beyond Jackson, but Sugar managed it, beautifully. He stepped out of his pants and sat down on the edge of the bed.

"Don't let me do anything you don't like, ever," he said, caressing the silky skin above her shorts. "I may not always ask first, but if I start something that makes you uncomfortable, all you have to say is no."

Sugar answered with a softly spoken agreement, but in her heart she knew if he would just kiss her again, everything would be all right. The kiss he gave her, though, was not the one she had expected.

Curling his fingers around her waistband, he drew her shorts down and lowered his mouth to her mons. His tongue slid up her cleft again and again until she melted into a shower of falling stars. Then he moved up her body to take her mouth with his as he began to take her virginity. His shaft was rigid, pulsing, probing her secret core, creating and easing an ache she couldn't escape.

His name fell from her lips over and over. She covered his face with sweet, hot kisses. His hair flowed around them and trailed across her breasts like tendrils of silken fire. Every atom of her being was alive and focused on the man sliding into her body.

A single thrust broke her barrier. She gasped a cry, which he caught with his kiss and took inside himself.

"Ah, Sugar." He crooned her name and whispered little nothings in her ear, words of pleasure and anticipation, of gentleness and caring and love.

He pumped slowly at first, easing his way inside before beginning a careful withdrawal. His eyes drifted closed on a heavenly sigh, layering thick lashes across his cheeks, and a lazy smile graced his mouth.

"You feel so good." The words were labored, husky. "So good." He opened his eyes and his smile broadened. "I could do this the rest of the day, but I don't think you'd thank me for that, not the first time."

She wasn't so sure. She'd never known any pleasure as great as the one of just watching him—the flowing movement of his hair over his shoulders and across her chest, the flexing of the muscles in his arms, the tightening of his abdomen, watching where they joined with his much larger, darker body meeting hers again and again.

Then something in her quickened, and she felt a

pleasure beyond the enticingly visual. Sensation deep inside her stirred, a desire for more with every stroke he made. Her gaze lifted to his face, and she watched the beautiful planes and angles there tauten with the same need for completion that drove her.

She had known she would give herself to this man. What she had not known was all he would give in return.

Her heart filled with love as wave upon wave of her climax washed through her. He came into her one last time in a shattering release, and she gathered him in her arms, the better to hold him and feel all the magic they had made.

Sated, breathing heavily, Jackson shifted his body off hers, taking as much weight as he could on his arms. She was so small and yet so powerful. She made him tremble.

He'd probably been too rough, but she had completely undone him and his good intentions.

"I'm sorry I hurt you." He lifted his hand and brushed strands of his hair off her cheek and out of her eyelashes. Thanks to him they were completely wrapped up in each other.

"You didn't hurt me, Jackson." Her smile was weak. She was limp beneath him. "At least not much."

"It will be better next time."

"How many next times do I get?" She opened her eyes for him, and they were fathomless, more enchanted than the lunar mists of Cocorico.

"A lifetime of next times, Sugar," he said, bending

his head to brush a kiss across her brow. "And then one more time after that."

FIFTEEN

Jackson stood in the San Francisco jungle yard of his sister-in-law's brother's house. As he watched his wife beguile the man with her knowledge of the bifurcation points of indigenous tropical species, he wondered at the changes three months of assumed death had brought to his life.

One thing was for damn certain, when death hovered nearby, people took love a lot more seriously. Both he and Cooper had ended up married, after years of globe-spanning bachelorhood.

Well, not so many years for him. He was only twenty-four. Conceivably, he could have been facing another decade of footlooseness. He'd gotten lucky instead and found his woman on a West Indian island half a world away from anyplace he ever would have dreamed of looking.

Cooper came over and, as he'd been prone to lately, gave Jackson a hug, a big hug of the bear variety.

"Hey, Coop." He delicately extricated himself from his big brother's arms. Truth was, he'd about had his fill of being hugged and coddled, except for the stuff Sugar dished out. He couldn't seem to get enough of that.

"Jessie and I have been talking," Cooper said, referring to his wife. "You and Sugar ought to have the beach house. With the kids and all, we really need something bigger and closer to town."

"Okay," Jackson said. It was another of those amazing changes, he mused, Cooper being a ready-made dad, with Jessie having two children from her first marriage. Of course, Jackson knew from personal experience that his big brother made a helluva father; he'd had lots of practice, having survived Jackson's hooligan years.

"We might even move into the suburbs," Cooper went on.

Things were really changing when they allowed the Dragon to move into the suburbs, Jackson thought, but all he said was, "We're not there that much, so take your time about finding a place. There's no hurry or anything."

Cooper slanted him a wry look. "Not unless I don't want the kids to grow up thinking married people spend all their time locked in the bedroom."

Jackson just grinned.

Cooper grew serious then. "There's something I wanted to talk to you about."

"If this is the big sex talk you were always supposed to give me, you're a little late, Coop. I already figured it out."

Cooper at least lightened up enough to smile. "No. It's about spending more time in California, both of us, cutting back our overseas interests, maybe getting more into the investment side of the business."

Jackson had seen this one coming for days. Cooper had hardly let him out of his sight. "I was never dead, Cooper. She didn't get me. She only got close, and close doesn't count."

"With Baolian everything counts. I want you out of her sight, out of her way."

Jackson kept his silence. He couldn't give Cooper that, not even close. He wasn't going to get out of Baolian's way. He was going to get in her face and back the Dragon Whore down whatever hole she'd crawled out of. He was a bounty hunter, and until he got Baolian, she was his prey.

"I know what you're thinking," Cooper said, "and it can't be done, not with any safeguards, maybe not even without. Besides, you're married now. You have to think about Sugar."

He was married, not dead, and he *was* thinking about Sugar.

"Okay, Coop," he said, cutting the conversation short with a smile and a wave as he headed across the yard.

When Sugar saw him coming, she excused herself from Paul, Jessie's gardening brother.

"What did you and Cooper find out this morning?" she asked.

Before he answered, he wrapped her in his arms and kissed the top of her head.

"You're going to get about ten grand for Sher Chang, and Jen and I come out at about twelve grand apiece, less expenses. That is, if he ever shows up to claim it." The old Chinaman had left the Kingstown Inn before she and Jackson had returned. He hadn't left a forwarding address, but they both knew he'd gone back to Shulan.

"What about Cocorico?" She missed her home, but not as much as she would have missed Jackson if she hadn't been with him.

"Cooper thinks we can go back with a few precautions, and I agree. The place really is inaccessible. A few communication adjustments and some protection would make a big difference in its integrity."

"Cocorico has always had impeccable integrity," she said, taking mock offense. "At least until you got there and started taking your clothes off."

"Hey, that's an idea." He grinned down at her.

"What?"

"We could go home and take our clothes off." He expected her to blush, but he should have known better. The woman didn't have a blush left in her.

Or did she?

He bent down and whispered in her ear, and sure enough, after a minute, he got her to blush.

"You're kidding," she said, slanting him a wary look.

"Scout's honor." He gave her the Boy Scout sign. "That's why they call it the 'kiss of death.'"

Her blush deepened, then a grin twitched her lips. "Do you love me?"

"More than I should."

Her grin broadened. "Do you trust me?"

Now it was his turn to give her a wary look. "Just enough . . . maybe."

"Chicken," she taunted, and he lunged, grabbing her and swinging her in close.

"I'm going to remember that later," he threatened her, but she gave as good as she got.

"I'm counting on it."

Moonlight filtered in through the sheer curtains and shone across the futon where they lay, safe and secure in each other's arms. Sugar looked over at her husband, enjoying the beauty of him in sleep.

He was a wild one, probably more than she could handle once he got back up to speed, if the contents of his room were any indication. They made a fine pair, with him old in the ways of the world and young at heart, and her with her ancient heart and being so young when it came to worldly things.

"Sugar?" he said drowsily, rolling on his side toward her.

"Hmm?"

In answer, he pulled her closer and promptly fell back asleep.

She loved him, loved him like no other before him, and she felt her love being returned with every breath he took.

YOU'VE READ THE BOOK.
NOW DOUBLE YOUR FUN BY ENTERING LOVESWEPT'S TREASURED TALES III CONTEST!

Everybody loves a good romance, especially when that romance is inspired by a beloved fairy tale, legend, even a Shakespearean play. It's an entertaining challenge for the writer to create a contemporary retelling of a classic story—and for you, the reader, to find the similarities between the retold story and the classic.

For example:
- While reading STALKING THE GIANT by Victoria Leigh, did you notice that the heroine's nickname is exactly the same as the giant-slayer's in "Jack and the Beanstalk"?
- How about the fact that, like Adam and Eve, the hero and heroine in Glenna McReynold's DRAGON'S EDEN are alone in a paradise setting?
- Surely the heroine's red cape in HOT SOUTHERN NIGHTS by Patt Bucheister reminded you of the one Little Red Riding Hood wears on the way to her grandma's house.
- You couldn't have missed the heroine's rebuffing of the hero in Peggy Webb's CAN'T STOP LOVING YOU. Kate, in Shakespeare's *Taming of the Shrew*, displays the same steeliness when dealing with Petruchio.

The four TREASURED TALES III romances this month contain many, many more wonderful similarities to the classic stories they're based on. And with LOVESWEPT'S TREASURED TALES III CONTEST, you have a once-in-a-lifetime opportunity to let us know how many of these similarities you found. Even better, because this is LOVESWEPT's third year of publishing TREASURED TALES, this contest will have **three winners!**

Read the Official Rules to find out what you need to do to enter LOVESWEPT'S TREASURED TALES III CONTEST.

Now, indulge in the magic of TREASURED TALES III —and grab a chance to win some treasures of your own!

LOVESWEPT'S TREASURED TALES III CONTEST

OFFICIAL RULES:

1. *No purchase is necessary.* Enter by printing or typing your name, address, and telephone number at the top of one (or more, if necessary) piece(s) of 8½" X 11" plain white paper, if typed, or lined paper, if handwritten. Then list each of the similarities you found in one or more of the TREASURED TALES III romances to the classic story each is based on. The romances are STALKING THE GIANT by Victoria Leigh (based on "Jack and the Beanstalk"), DRAGON'S EDEN by Glenna McReynolds (based on "Adam and Eve"), HOT SOUTHERN NIGHTS by Patt Bucheister (based on "Little Red Riding Hood"), and CAN'T STOP LOVING YOU by Peggy Webb (based on *Taming of the Shrew*). Each book is available in libraries. Please be sure to list the similarities found below the title of the romance(s) read. Also, for use by the judges in case of a tie, write an essay of 150 words or less stating why you like to read LOVESWEPT romances. Once you've finished your list and your essay, mail your entry to: LOVESWEPT'S TREASURED TALES III CONTEST, Dept. BdG, Bantam Books, 1540 Broadway, New York, NY 10036.

2. PRIZES (3): All three (3) winners will receive a six (6) months' subscription to the LOVESWEPT Book Club and twenty-one (21) autographed books. Each winner will also be featured in a one-page profile that will appear in the back of Bantam Books' LOVESWEPT'S TREASURED TALES IV romances, scheduled for publication in February 1996. (Approximate retail value: $200.00)

3. Contest entries must be postmarked and received by March 31, 1995, and all entrants must be 21 or older on the date of entry. The author of each romance featured in LOVESWEPT'S TREASURED TALES III has provided a list of the similarities between her romance and the classic story it is based on. Entrants need not read all four TREASURED TALES III romances to enter, but the more they read, the more similarities they are likely to find. The entries submitted will be judged by members of the LOVESWEPT Editorial Staff, who will first count up the number of similarities each entrant identified, then compare the similarities found by the entrants who identified the most with the similarities listed by the author of the romance or romances read by those entrants and select the three entrants who correctly identified the greatest number of similarities. If more than three entrants correctly identify the greatest number, the judges will read the essays submitted by each potential winner in order to break the tie and select the entrants who submitted the best essays as the prize winners. The essays will be judged on the basis of the originality, creativity, thoughtfulness, and writing ability shown. All of the judges' decisions are final and binding. All essays must be original. Entries become the property of Bantam Books and will not be returned. Bantam Books is not responsible for incomplete or lost or misdirected entries.

4. Winners will be notified by mail on or about June 15, 1995. Winners have 30 days from the date of notice in which to claim their prize or an alternate winner will be chosen. Odds of winning are dependent on the number of entries received. Prizes are non-transferable and no substitutions are allowed. Winners may be required to execute an Affidavit Of Eligibility And Promotional Release supplied by Bantam Books and will need to supply a photograph of themselves for inclusion in the one-page profile of each winner. Entering the Contest constitutes permission for use of the winner's name, address (city and state), photograph, biographical profile, and Contest essay for publicity and promotional purposes, with no additional compensation.

5. Employees of Bantam Books, Bantam Doubleday Dell Publishing Group, Inc., their subsidiaries and affiliates, and their immediate family members are not eligible to enter. This Contest is open to residents of the U.S. and Canada, excluding the Province of Quebec, and is void wherever prohibited or restricted by law. Taxes, if any, are the winner's sole responsibility.

6. For a list of the winners, send a self-addressed, stamped envelope entirely separate from your entry to LOVESWEPT'S TREASURED TALES III CONTEST WINNERS LIST, Dept. BdG, Bantam Books, 1540 Broadway, New York, NY 10036. The list will be available after August 1, 1995.

THE EDITOR'S CORNER

With March comes gray, rainy days and long, cold nights, but here at LOVESWEPT things are really heating up! The four terrific romances we have in store for you are full of emotion, humor, and passion, with sexy heroes and dazzling heroines you'll never forget. So get ready to treat yourself with next month's LOVESWEPTS—they'll definitely put you in the mood for spring.

Starting things off is the delightfully unique Olivia Rupprecht with **PISTOL IN HIS POCKET**, LOVESWEPT #730. Lori Morgan might dare to believe in a miracle, that a man trapped for decades in a glacier can be revived, but she knows she has no business falling in love with the rough-hewn hunk! Yet when Noble Zhivago draws a breath in her bathtub, she feels reckless enough to respond to the dark stranger who seizes her lips and pulls her into the water. Wooed with passion and purpose by a magnificent warrior who tantalizes her senses, Lori must admit to adoring a man with a dangerous past. Olivia delivers both sizzling sensuality and heartbreaking emotion in this uninhibited romp.

The wonderfully talented Janis Reams Hudson's hero is **CAUGHT IN THE ACT,** LOVESWEPT #731. Betrayed, bleeding, and on the run, Trace Youngblood needs a hiding place—but will Lillian Roberts be his downfall, or his deliverance? The feisty teacher probably believes he is guilty as sin, but he needs her help to clear his name. Drawn to the rugged agent who embodies her secret yearnings, Lillian trusts him with her life, but is afraid she won't escape with her heart. Funny and wild, playful and explosive, smart and sexy, this is definitely another winner from Janis.

Rising star Donna Kauffman offers a captivating heart-stopper with **WILD RAIN,** LOVESWEPT #732. Jillian Bonner insists she isn't leaving, no matter how fierce the tempest headed her way, but Reese Braedon has a job to do—even if it means tossing the sweet spitfire over his shoulder and carrying her off! When the storm traps them together, the sparks that flash between them threaten spontaneous combustion. But once he brands her with the fire of his deepest need, she might never let him go. With a hero as wild and unpredictable as a hurricane, and a heroine who matches him in courage, will, and humor, Donna delivers a tale of outlaws who'd risk anything for passion—and each other.

Last, but never least, is the ever-popular Judy Gill with **SIREN SONG,** LOVESWEPT #733. Returning after fifteen years to the isolated beach where orca whales come to play, Don Jacobs once more feels seduced—by the place, and by memories of a young girl who'd offered him her innocence, a gift he'd hungered for but had to refuse. Tracy Maxwell still bewitches him, but is this beguiling woman of secrets finally free to surrender her heart? This evocative story explores the sweet mystery of longing and passion as only Judy Gill can.

Happy reading!

With warmest wishes,

Beth de Guzman

Senior Editor

P.S. Don't miss the women's novels coming your way in March: **NIGHT SINS**, the first Bantam hardcover by bestselling author Tami Hoag is an electrifying, heart-pounding tale of romantic suspense; **THE FOREVER TREE** by Rosanne Bittner is an epic, romantic saga of California and the courageous men and women who built their dreams out of redwood timber in the bestselling western tradition of Louis L'Amour; **MY GUARDIAN ANGEL** is an enchanting collection of romantic stories featuring a "guardian angel" theme from some of Bantam's finest romance authors, including Kay Hooper, Elizabeth Thornton, Susan Krinard, and Sandra Chastain; **PAGAN BRIDE** by Tamara Leigh is a wonderful historical romance in the bestselling tradition of Julie Garwood and Teresa Medeiros. We'll be giving you a sneak peek at these terrific books in next month's LOVESWEPTs. And immediately following this page, look for a preview of the exciting romances from Bantam that are *available now!*

Don't miss these irresistible books by
your favorite Bantam authors

On sale in January:

VALENTINE
by Jane Feather

*PRINCE OF
DREAMS*
by Susan Krinard

FIRST LOVES
by Jean Stone

From the beguiling, bestselling author of *Vixen* and *Velvet* comes a tale brimming with intrigue and passion

VALENTINE
BY
Jane Feather

"An author to treasure."
—*Romantic Times*

A quirk of fate has made Sylvester Gilbraith the heir of his sworn enemy, the earl of Stoneridge. But there's a catch: to claim his inheritance he has to marry one of the earl's four granddaughters. The magnetically handsome nobleman has no choice but to comply with the terms of the will, yet when he descends on Stoneridge Manor prepared to charm his way into a fortune, he finds that the lady who intrigues him most has no intention of becoming his bride. Maddeningly beautiful and utterly impossible, Theodora Belmont refuses to admit to the chemistry between them, even when she's passionately locked in his embrace. Yet soon the day will come when the raven-haired vixen will give anything to be Sylvester's bride and risk everything to defend his honor . . . and his life.

"You take one step closer, my lord, and you'll go down those stairs on your back," Theo said. "And with any luck you'll break your neck in the process."

Sylvester shook his head. "I don't deny your skill, but mine is as good, and I have the advantage of size and strength." He saw the acknowledgment leap into her eyes, but her position didn't change.

"Let's have done with this," he said sharply. "I'm prepared to forget that silly business by the stream."

"Oh, are you, my lord? How very generous of you. As I recall, you were not the one insulted."

"As I recall, you, cousin, were making game of me. Now, come downstairs. I wish you to ride around the estate with me."

"You wish me to do *what*?" Theo stared at him, her eyes incredulous.

"I understand from your mother that you've had the management of the estate for the last three years," said impatiently, as if his request were the most natural imaginable. "You're the obvious person to show me around."

"You have windmills in your head, sir. I wouldn't give you the time of day!" Theo swung on her heel and made to continue up the stairs.

"You rag-mannered hoyden!" Sylvester exclaimed. "We may have started on the wrong foot, but there's no excuse for such incivility." He sprang after her, catching her around the waist.

She spun, one leg flashing in a high kick aimed at his chest, but as he'd warned her, this time he was ready for her. Twisting, he caught her body across his thighs, swinging a leg over hers, clamping them in a scissors grip between his knees.

"Now, yield!" he gritted through his teeth, adjusting his grip against the sinuous working of her muscles as she fought to free herself.

Theo went suddenly still, her body limp against him. Instinctively he relaxed his grip and the next instant she was free, bounding up the next flight of stairs.

Sylvester went after her, no longer capable of cool

reasoning. A primitive battle was raging and he knew only that he wasn't going to lose it. No matter that it was undignified and totally inappropriate.

Theo raced down the long corridor, hearing his booted feet pounding behind her in time with her thundering heart. She didn't know whether her heart was speeding with fear or exhilaration; she didn't seem capable of rational, coherent thought.

His breath was on the back of her neck as she wrenched open the door of her bedroom and leaped inside, but his foot went in the gap as she tried to slam the door shut. She leaned on the door with all her weight, but Sylvester put his shoulder against the outside and heaved. Theo went reeling into the room and the door swung wide.

Sylvester stepped inside, kicking the door shut behind him.

"Very well," Theo said breathlessly. "If you wish it, I'll apologize for being uncivil. I shouldn't have said what I did just now."

"For once we're in agreement," he remarked, coming toward her. Theo cast a wild look around the room. In a minute she was going to be backed up against the armoire and she didn't have too many tricks left.

Sylvester reached out and seized the long, thick rope of hair hanging down her back. He twisted it around his wrist, reeling her in like a fish until her face was on a level with his shoulder.

He examined her countenance as if he was seeing it for the first time. Her eyes had darkened and he could read the sparking challenge in their depths; a flush of exertion and emotion lay beneath the golden brown of her complexion and her lips were slightly parted, as if she was about to launch into another of her tirades.

To prevent such a thing, he tightened his grip on her plait, bringing her face hard against his shoulder, and kissed her.

Theo was so startled that she forgot about resistance for a split second, and in that second discovered that she was enjoying the sensation. Her lips parted beneath the probing thrust of his tongue and her own tongue touched his, at first tentatively, then with increasing confidence. She inhaled the scent of his skin, a sun-warmed earthy smell that was new to her. His mouth tasted of wine. His body was hard-muscled against her own, and when she stirred slightly she became startlingly aware of a stiffness in his loins. Instinctively she pressed her lower body against his.

Sylvester drew back abruptly, his eyes hooded as he looked down into her intent face. "I'll be damned," he muttered. "How many men have you kissed?"

"None," she said truthfully. Her anger had vanished completely, surprise and curiosity in its place. She wasn't even sure whether she still disliked him.

"I'll be damned," he said again, a slight smile tugging at the corners of his mouth, little glints of amusement sparking in the gray eyes. "I doubt you'll be a restful wife, cousin, but I'll lay odds you'll be full of surprises."

Theo remembered that she *did* dislike him . . . intensely. She twitched her plait out of his slackened grip and stepped back. "I fail to see what business that is of yours, Lord Stoneridge."

"Ah, yes, I was forgetting we haven't discussed this as yet," he said, folding his arms, regarding her with deepening amusement. "We're going to be married, you and I."

PRINCE OF DREAMS
BY
Susan Krinard

San Francisco psychologist Diana Ransom can't take her eyes off the gorgeous, green-eyed stranger. But when she finally approaches him across the smoke-filled room, her reasons have little to do with the treacherous feelings he inspires. Diana suspects that this brooding, enigmatic man is responsible for the disappearance of her young cousin. Desperate to find her, and determined to plumb the mystery behind Nicholas Gale's hypnotic charm, Diana will follow him into the velvety darkness . . . and awake to a haunting passion. For Nicholas is no mere human, but a vampire with the power to steal into a woman's dreams and fill her nights with untold rapture. And soon, blinded by an ecstasy sweeter than any she's ever known, Diana will find herself risking her eternal soul for a love that promises to be forever. . . .

For a moment the woman across the table was no more than a jumble of colors and heat and flaring life force. Nicholas struggled to focus on her face, on her stubborn, intelligent eyes.

He said the first thing that came into his head. "Do you have a first name, Dr. Ransom?"

She blinked at him, caught off guard and resentful of it. "I don't see what that has to do with Keely or where she is, Mr. Gale. That's all I'm interested in at the moment. If you—"

"Then we're back to where we started, Dr. Ransom. As it happens, I share your concern for Keely." He lost his train of thought for a moment, looking at the woman with her brittle control and overwhelming aura. He could almost hear the singing of her life force in the three feet of space between them.

He nearly reached out to touch her. Just to see what she would feel like, if that psychic energy would flow into him with so simple a joining.

He stopped his hand halfway across the table and clenched it carefully. She had never seen him move.

"What *is* your business, Mr. Gale?" she asked. The antagonism in her voice had grown muted, and there was a flicker of uncertainty in her eyes.

"I have many varied . . . interests," he said honestly. He smiled, and for a moment he loosed a tiny part of his hunter's power.

She stared at him and lifted a small hand to run her fingers through her short brown hair, effectively disordering the loose curls. That simple act affected Nicholas with unexpected power. He felt his groin tighten, a physical response he had learned to control and ignore long ago.

When was the last time? he asked himself. The last time he had lain with a woman, joined with her physically, taken some part of what he needed in the act of love?

Before he could blunt the thought, his imagination slipped its bonds, conjuring up an image of this woman, her aura ablaze, naked and willing and fully conscious beneath him. Knowing what he was, giving and receiving without fear. . . .

"Diana."

"What?" Reality ripped through Nicholas, dispelling the erotic, impossible vision.

"My first name is Diana," she murmured.

Her face was flushed, as if she had seen the lust in his eyes. She was an attractive woman. Mortal men would pursue her, even blind to her aura as they must be. Did she look at him and observe only another predictable male response to be dissected with an analyst's detachment?

His hungers were not so simple. He would have given the world to make them so.

"Diana," he repeated softly. "Huntress, and goddess of the moon."

She wet her lips. "It's getting late, Mr. Gale—"

"*My* first name is Nicholas."

"Nicholas," she echoed, as if by rote. "I'll be making a few more inquiries about Keely. If you were serious about being concerned for her—"

"I was."

Diana twisted around in her chair and lifted a small, neat purse. "Here," she said, slipping a card from a silver case. "This is where you can reach me if you should hear from her."

Nicholas took the card and examined the utilitarian printing. *Diana Ransom, Ph.D. Licensed Psychologist. Individual psychotherapy. Treatment of depression, anxiety, phobias, and related sleep disorders.*

Sleep disorders. Nicholas almost smiled at the irony of it. She could never cure his particular disorder. He looked up at her. "If you need to talk to me again, I'm here most nights."

"Then you don't plan to leave town in the next few days?" she asked with a touch of her former hostility.

His gaze was steady. "No, Diana. I'll make a few inquiries of my own."

They stared at each other. *Diana*. Was she a child of the night, as her name implied? Did she dream vivid dreams that he could enter as he could never enter her body? Or was she part of the sane and solid world of daylight, oblivious to the untapped power that sang in her aura like a beacon in darkness?

She was the first to look away. Hitching the strap of her purse higher on her shoulder, she rose. "Then I'll be going." She hesitated, slanting a look back at him with narrowed blue eyes. "Perhaps we'll see each other again . . . Nicholas."

He watched her walk away and up the stairs. Her words had held a warning. No promise, no hint of flirtation. With even a little effort he could have won her over. He could have learned more about her, perhaps enough to determine if she would be a suitable candidate to serve his needs. One glimpse of her aura was enough to tempt him almost beyond reason.

But she had affected him too deeply. He could not afford even the slightest loss of control with his dreamers. Emotional detachment was a matter of survival—his and that of the women he touched by night.

Diana Ransom was something almost beyond his experience—.

Although he would never sample the promise behind Diana Ransom's unremarkable façade, would never slip into her dreams and skim the abundance of energy that burned beneath her skin. . . .

As he had done a thousand times before, Nicholas schooled himself to detachment and consigned hope and memory to their familiar prisons. If he arranged matters correctly, he need never see Diana Ransom again.

What if you could go back and rediscover
the magic . . . ?

FIRST LOVES
BY
Jean Stone

*For every woman there is a first love, the love she never
forgets. You always wonder what would have happened,
what might have been. Here is a novel of three women
with the courage to go back . . . but could they recover
the magic they left behind?*

"Men," Alissa said. "They really are scum, you
know."

"Maybe it's partly our fault," Meg replied quietly.

"Are you nuts?" Alissa asked. "Besides, how
would you know? You're not even married." She took
a sip of wine. "Bet you have a boyfriend, though.
Some equally successful power attorney, perhaps? Or
maybe that private investigator? What was his
name?"

"His name is Danny. And no, he's only a friend. A
good friend. But right now, there's no one special in
my life."

Alissa set down her glass. "See? If someone as
beautiful and clever and smart as you doesn't have a
boyfriend, it proves they're all scum. I rest my case."

Though she knew Alissa's words could be considered a compliment, Meg suddenly found old feelings
resurfacing, the feelings of being the kid with no fa-

ther, the one who was different, inadequate. "I've had a lot of boyfriends—men friends," she stuttered.

"But how about relationships?" Alissa pressed. "*Real* relationships?"

In her mind Meg saw his face, his eyes, his lips. She felt his touch. "Once," she replied quietly, "a long time ago."

Alissa leaned back in her chair. "Yeah, I guess you could say I had one once, too. But it sure as shit wasn't with my husband. It was before him." She drained her glass and poured another. "God, it was good."

Meg was relieved to have the focus of the conversation off herself. "What happened?"

"His name was Jay. Jay Stockwell. Our parents had summer homes next to each other."

"You were childhood sweethearts?" Zoe asked, then added wistfully, "I think they're the best. Everyone involved is so innocent."

Alissa shook her head. "This wasn't innocence. It was love. Real love."

They grew quiet. Meg thought of Steven Riley, about their affair. That was love. Real love. But it was years ago. A lifetime ago.

The waiter arrived and set their dinners on the red paper placemats. Meg stared at the cheeseburger. Suddenly she had no appetite.

After he left, Zoe spoke. "What is real love, anyway? How do you know? William took good care of me and of Scott. But I can't honestly say I loved him. Not like I'd loved the boy back home."

"Ah," Alissa said, "the boy back home. For me, that was Jay. The trouble was, he didn't want to stay home. He had things to do, a world to save."

"Where did he go?"

Meg was glad Zoe was keeping Alissa talking. She

could feel herself sliding into the lonely depression of thoughts of Steven. She could feel her walls closing around her, her need to escape into herself. For some reason she thought about the cat she'd had then—a gray tiger named Socrates. For the longest time after Steven was gone she'd closed Socrates out of her bedroom. She'd not been able to stand hearing him purr; the sound was too close to the soft snores of Steven beside her, at peace in his slumber after their love-making.

"First, Jay went to San Francisco," Alissa was saying, and Meg snapped back to the present. "It was in the early seventies. He'd been deferred from the draft. From Vietnam."

"Was he sick?" Zoe asked.

"No," Alissa said. "He was rich. Rich boys didn't have to go. Jay's family owned—and still do—a mega-broadcast conglomerate. TV stations. Radio stations. All over the country. Jay loved broadcasting, but not business. He was a born journalist." She pushed the plate with her untouched cheeseburger and fries aside. "When he went to San Francisco, he gave his family the finger."

"And you never saw him again?" Zoe asked.

Alissa laughed. "Never saw him again? Darling," she said, as she took another sip of wine, "I went with him."

"You went with him?" Even Meg was surprised at this. She couldn't picture Alissa following anyone, anywhere.

"I was eighteen. Love seemed more important than trust funds or appearances or social standing."

"So what happened?" Zoe asked.

She shrugged. "I realized I was wrong."

The women were quiet. Meg felt sorry for Alissa. Something in the eyes of this tiny, busy, aggressive little blonde now spelled sorrow. Sorrow for a life gone by. Sorrow for love relinquished. She knew the feeling only too well.

"God, he was handsome," Alissa said. "He still is."

"Still is?" Zoe asked. "You mean you still see him?"

Alissa shook her head. "I left him standing at the corner of Haight and Ashbury. It seemed appropriate at the time. He was working for one of those liberal underground newspapers. I went home to Atlanta, married Robert, had the kids. Then one day I turned on the TV and there he was. Reporting from Cairo."

"So he went back into broadcasting," Zoe said.

"Full steam ahead, apparently. Delivering stories on the oppressed peoples of the world. Over the years I've seen him standing against backdrops in Lebanon, Ethiopia, Iraq, you name it. He was on the air for days during that Tiananmen Square thing in China or wherever that is."

"Oh," Zoe said, "Jay Stockwell. Sure. I've seen him, too. His stories have real sensitivity."

Alissa shrugged. "I never paid much attention to his stories. I was too busy looking at him. Wondering."

Zoe picked at her scallops, then set down her fork. "Wondering what would have happened if you'd stayed together?"

"Sure. Haven't you ever done that? Wondered about your boy back home?"

"You mean, the man I could have married?" Zoe asked.

"Or should have," Alissa said.

Should have, Meg thought. Should I have? Could I have?

"Sure I've wondered about him," Zoe said. "All the time."

"What about you, Meg? What about your one and only? Don't you ever wonder how your life would have been different. How it would have been better?"

Meg silently wished she could say, "No. My life wouldn't have been better. It would have been worse. And besides, my life is just fine the way it is." But she couldn't seem to say anything. She couldn't seem to lie.

There was silence around the table. Meg looked at Zoe, who was watching Alissa. Meg turned to Alissa, just in time to see her quickly wipe a lone tear from her cheek. Alissa caught Meg's eye and quickly cleared her throat. Then she raised her glass toward them both. "I think we should find them," Alissa said. "I think we should find the men we once loved, and show them what they've missed."

And don't miss these fabulous romances
from Bantam Books,
on sale in February:

NIGHT SINS
Available in hardcover
by the nationally bestselling author

Tami Hoag

THE FOREVER TREE
by the award-winning

Rosanne Bittner

PAGAN BRIDE
by the highly acclaimed

Tamara Leigh

"MY GUARDIAN ANGEL"
anthology featuring:

Sandra Chastain   Kay Hooper
Susan Krinard   Karyn Monk
Elizabeth Thornton